Wisconsin:

Book Two

Promise Me Forever

As the Founder/CEO of NAVH, the only national health agency solely devoted to those who, although not totally blind, have an eye disease which could lead to serious visual impairment, I am pleased to recognize Thorndike Press★ as one of the leading publishers in the large print field.

Founded in 1954 in San Francisco to prepare large print textbooks for partially seeing children, NAVH became the pioneer and standard setting agency in the preparation of large type.

Today, those publishers who meet our standards carry the prestigious "Seal of Approval" indicating high quality large print. We are delighted that Thorndike Press is one of the publishers whose titles meet these standards. We are also pleased to recognize the significant contribution Thorndike Press is making in this important and growing field.

Lorraine H. Marchi, L.H.D.
Founder/CEO
NAVH

★Thorndike Press encompasses the following imprints: Thorndike, Wheeler, Walker and Large Print Press.

Prologue

June 16

The little country chapel in Lyon, Illinois, was modestly, but tastefully decorated. Fresh floral arrangements stood in glass vases, white roses tied with emerald bows, near the altar and pleated paper wedding bells hung about. The pews were filled with enthusiastic friends and relatives who had come to share this special day. A wedding day, uniting for life Julia Rose McGowan and Mark Thomas Henley.

In the small dressing room in back of the chapel, Julia smoothed the skirt of her formal white lace gown which her Aunt Louise had sewn especially for this day.

"You look beautiful, dear," Julia's mother, Caroline, said with a proud smile. Then tears gathered in her green eyes. "You're the most beautiful bride I've ever seen."

"Oh, Mom, don't cry," Julia chided her gently. "You'll ruin your makeup. Don't forget pictures afterward in the park across the street."

Nodding, Caroline dabbed her eyes with a tissue. Her dark auburn hair, streaked with strands of gray, had been swept up in a regal bun.

"Can you believe it, Juli?" her best friend and maid of honor, Kathy, asked. The slim brunette fussed over Julia's lacy veil. "You and Mark ——. married." Kathy sighed, looking dreamy. "What a fairy tale. High school sweethearts, married forever!"

Julia was smiling, too. She had been in love with Mark Henley ever since the Junior Prom —— that was two years ago. Julia was eighteen years old now and had just graduated from high school last month. Mark was a year older and, though some people said they were too young to make a life-long commitment to each other, Julia and Mark knew they were so much in love that it didn't matter. They promised each other that together they would conquer any obstacles brought on or compounded by their youth. After all, they had each other ... what more did they need?

"I'm glad that we'll be sisters," Teri Henley said. Blond like her brother, she was sixteen years old and one of Julia's bridesmaids.

"I'm doubly glad!" declared fifteen-year-old Jenny Henley. "Now we've got the Henley men outnumbered!" She smeared gloss on her lips, then tugged at the forest green bridesmaid dress she wore.

"Yeah, it was a draw before. Mom, Jenny, and me, Tim, Mark and Dad, that is, before Dad left."

At Teri's words a cloud of despair seemed to settle over the room.

"What on Earth makes a man go so crazy that he up and leaves his wife and kids for some other younger woman and a job transfer to Oregon?" Teri continued.

Julia shook her head sadly. "I don't know, Teri. A mid-life crisis, maybe."

"Now, let's not spoil this special day with troubled thoughts and grim speculations, all right?" Caroline McGowan smiled at her daughter first and then at the Henley sisters. "This is a happy occasion, and there isn't a thing you can do about your dad today."

"But he wouldn't even come for Mark's wedding," Jenny said with a large pout.

"His loss!" Julia exclaimed. She was angry with Mark's father for what he had done to his family. It was a scandalous thing, especially in this close-knit, rural community in central Illinois.

9

Kathy suddenly held out a tube of pink lipstick. "~~I think~~ you need some of this so when Reverend Ritter tells the groom 'You may kiss the bride' you can smooch Pink Passion all over Mark's face." She laughed. "That'll make a great wedding picture!"

"Okay." With an impish grin, Julia turned to the mirror and smoothed on the lipstick. Then she rubbed her lips together.

"Oh, that's a pretty color," Caroline remarked.

"Yeah," said Kathy, "it'll look great on Mark, too!"

Giggles went around the room. Then, minutes later, the females in their lace and satin ruffles, left the room to line up for the procession as planned at the previous night's rehearsal.

Julia's father was already waiting in the vestibule, wearing a light grey tuxedo. He looked so handsome out of his greasy work clothes that Julia's eyes grew misty. Her daddy all dressed up to give her away.

Suddenly Tim Henley, Mark's older brother appeared. He seemed anxious.

"You okay, Tim?" Julia asked.

He took a deep breath. "I've got to speak with you," he said in hushed tones. "It's important."

"But the wedding march is going to start and —"

"Juli, really —"

She looked at him with a concerned frown, but then nodded. "All right."

Lifting her hem slightly, Julia followed Tim away from her parents and bridesmaids and back to the far corner of the vestibule.

"What is it?"

"It's Mark."

"Mark?"

Tim nodded. "He's gone, Julia."

Her eyes widened. "Gone?" She didn't understand. "What do you mean gone?"

Again, Tim took a deep breath. "Juli, he called me from the airport about half an hour ago." He looked down at his rented tux then. Blond and blue-eyed like Mark, he had been chosen as the best man. "I didn't know what to do."

"What?" Julia's head began to spin. "What are you talking about?"

Tim pulled a letter from out of the inside pocket of his jacket. "I think this will explain everything," he said in a gentle voice. "Mark wrote it last night. After the rehearsal dinner. I found it in my tux pocket after he called."

11

Tears filled Julia's eyes as she unfolded the sheet of lined notebook paper. She read:

Dear Juli,

I can't go through with it. I'm not ready for the altar. I can't work at a gas station the rest of my life! I wouldn't be able to stand it! I appreciate your dad giving me the job, but I want to do more with my life. My dad was right when he said I'd never be happy working as a greasy auto mechanic forever. And it's true. I want a career. Like the one Dad has, working for one of the biggest insurance companies in the nation.

But I know my mom won't understand. She's a romantic. She always said, "love never fails," but, considering her and Dad, I guess it did anyway.

Maybe marriage isn't such a good thing, Juli-bean. My sweet, sweet Juli-bean. I promise I'll always love you, but I'd probably end up breaking your heart . . . just like my old man did to my mom. Just like I'm doing right now.

A sob escaped from the innermost part of Julia's being and she let the letter slip from her fingers. It fell to the worn,

12

wooden floor of the old chapel along with the first of many tears.

"Mark went to live with my dad in Oregon," Tim informed her in somber tones. "He's decided to go to college. Dad said he'd pay for it if Mark called off the wedding."

The news was as crushing to Julia's heart as an iron wrecking ball to a fragile, crystal champagne glass. Mark. Julia loved him so! So much, in fact, she had given him the most precious thing a woman could ever give a man herself.

"What's going on here?" Roy McGowan asked, suddenly standing beside his daughter. He put a parental arm around her. "What's happened, Julia?"

"It's M–Mark," she sobbed, turning and throwing her arms around her father's neck. "He left me, Dad!" she cried into the shoulder of his tuxedo. "He left me!"

Fifteen minutes later, the father of the bride walked up and stood before the guests. His shoulders sagged as he made the sad announcement. "Dear friends," he began, "I'm afraid there's not going to be a wedding today."

Chapter 1

June 17 — twelve years later

The alarm startled Julia awake at five-thirty. She rolled over sleepily and shut it off. Then, yawning and stretching, she crawled out of bed and padded to the windows. Peonies, she thought, spotting the abundance of pink and white bushes lining the tennis courts. It's late springtime when the peonies are in bloom.

The past month had been so rainy and cold that Julia was almost hoping spring would never come — as if the seasons could pass from winter right into summer. Late spring was not pleasant for Julia, at least it hadn't been for the last twelve years. Once it had been her favorite time of year, but it was now a difficult season to endure. Peonies and spring brought to mind a certain wedding day so long ago — and a ceremony that never took place. It was twelve years ago yesterday.

Turning from the windows, Julia shook off her melancholy, changed into her nylon windsuit and began her habitual morning jog. She forced herself to count her many blessings and, of course, Jesse was one of them. At eleven years old, her son meant the world to Julia, and if she hurried, she would be back at their apartment before he awoke.

After Mark Henley left her for a college education and ideas about a fabulous career, Julia discovered that she was pregnant. Her parents were terribly disappointed in her, and Julia felt so ashamed. She had known her intimacy with Mark was wrong, but she convinced herself that since they were getting married it was all right. It wasn't. And, consequently, Julia found herself alone and in a terrible predicament.

Finally the decision was made that, to avoid a scandal in their small-town community, Julia would go to live with relatives: Barb and Glen French who resided in Menomonee Falls, Wisconsin. The plan was that Julia would put her baby up for adoption; however, after Jesse was born, she couldn't bear to part with him. He was, after all, the result of her intense love for Mark—even though Mark never knew about the baby. Neither did his family who had moved to Springfield to escape the gossip surrounding Mark's father's absence.

Stop dwelling on the past! she chided herself. But between Jesse and the time of year, the reprimand seemed preposterous. She could no more stop thinking about Mark Henley right now than she could stop breathing.

Re-entering the apartment, Julia poured herself a generous glass of orange juice. "Jesse, it's time to get up," she called as she turned on the television.

Then, while her son, blond and blue-eyed, stumbled to the kitchen and sleepily poured himself a bowl of cereal, Julia showered. By seven o'clock, she was dressed in a smart yellow silk blouse, black linen skirt, and black and yellow checkered linen jacket. Slipping into black pumps, Julia returned to the bathroom where she pinned up her shoulder-length, wavy, auburn hair. Then she applied a subtle amount of makeup — just enough to accentuate her teal-blue eyes. With a hand mirror, she considered her reflection and nodded with satisfaction. She looked businesslike. Professional.

"What time are you coming to get me at

Aunt Barb and Uncle Glen's house?" Jesse asked. He had pulled on blue jeans and a red polo shirt.

"About eight-thirty," Julia replied. "I'm still working on that computer program for Customer Service."

"You'll get it right, Mom, don't worry," Jesse said with a confident look on his face.

Julia smiled. "You have more faith in me than my associates do, Jess." She gave him a curious look then. "Speaking of faith . . . did you have your devotions this morning?"

"Nope, but I'm going to do them with Uncle Glen. We pray together, too."

Julia nodded, though she felt the pinch of hypocrisy. When was the last time she'd had her devotions? Much to her dismay, Julia couldn't even remember. Lately God seemed far away, although it hadn't always been that way.

Before Jesse was born, Barb helped Julia come to a saving knowledge of Christ. She had been so excited about it, too. Forgiveness. No more guilt and shame over past sins. She was forgiven! And it was as if she could feel God's presence in every aspect of her life. It was exciting.

Then Julia had shared her newly found faith with her parents and brothers, and they too became Christians — all except for her father, that is. She was still praying for him. They all were. And Jesse ... he was a special boy. At least, Julia thought so. He had understood his need for the Savior when he was just six years old.

"C'mon, Mom," he was calling from the side door. "I'll race you to the car!"

Laughing together, mother and son ran from their apartment to the hunter green, Buick Park Avenue which was housed in a heated garage under all the units.

"I win!" Julia teased.

"No way. I got to the car first!" Jesse cried.

Julia had to laugh, knowing she had lost, fair and square. Unlocking the car door, she climbed in and opened the passenger side for Jesse. They drove the distance to the Frenches' home on the north side of Menomonee Falls and, by eight o'clock, Julia was entering the well-groomed property of Weakland Capital Management Corporation.

As Julia drove into her assigned parking slot and then entered the double glass doors of Weakland Management, she mentally prepared herself for her role as Manager of Information Systems. At work, Julia was cool — if not distant — but polite, intelligent, and always a professional. Relationships, she had learned, were risky, especially at work — especially in her position. Distance, she had discovered, was safe.

Julia's heels clicked smartly on the tile flooring now, as she walked through the women's locker area, and her stomach growled as she headed toward the cafeteria-style restaurant. Already she could smell the delicious aromas coming from its kitchen.

"Good morning, Juli," Stacie Rollins, the manager of Customer Service, said with a little smile. "I sincerely hope your people are going to have my program up and running today. It's been a horrible mess since Thursday."

"Conversions usually are." Julia stepped in beside Stacie and waited to place her order with Walter, the proprietor — or "Sir Walter" as he was fondly referred to at Weakland Management. He was from England and frequently entertained employees with his tales of London, during which his accent became more apparent than ever. However, his abilities in the kitchen were far more impressive than his English accent.

Julia ordered an egg bagel, strawberry

cream cheese, half of a grapefruit and a serving of strawberries for her breakfast. Stacie ordered bacon and eggs.

"May I join you?" she asked, after Julia had taken her usual place in the dining room. Julia was fond of sitting next to the windows where she could look out over the vast gardens and evergreens behind the little pond while she ate.

Looking at Stacie, now, she simply nodded.

"Have you heard the latest?" Stacie asked, lifting a well-sculptured blond brow. "Bill has hired a consultant."

Julia nodded. "I heard."

Stacie looked surprised. "When?"

Julia just smiled. "Late Friday afternoon. Bill told me."

Stacie swallowed her obvious indignation at not being the first to hear. "Well," she said, shaking out her napkin and setting it in her lap, "I think it's a preposterous idea. We don't need a consultant around here. Everything is running smoothly." Stacie gave Julia a pointed look. "Except for my computer program, that is."

Julia chuckled softly. "We'll get it right. Don't worry. It's an excellent program. I think you're going to be very pleased. Give us a chance."

"Do I have a choice?"

Julia shrugged, though she detected a hint of a smile on Stacie's full, red lips. But she wasn't too concerned with Stacie's criticisms. Bill Weakland, the CEO and president, had been impressed with Julia's presentation of the new Customer Service computer program.

"Well, anyway, I met him this morning."

"Who?" Julia asked, distracted by her breakfast and thoughts of computer programming.

"The business consultant. I met him this morning." Stacie rolled her eyes and gave Julia a look as if to say, Pay attention, will you?

Smiling inwardly, Julia asked, "What are your first impressions?"

Stacie seemed eager to give them. "He's tall, blond, blue eyes, broad shoulders—Evan Picone and Lagerfeld all the way."

Julia couldn't help an amused grin. "Don't underestimate our new consultant, Stacie. Underneath those popular name brands is a man to be respected. I mean, Bill wouldn't have hired him if he wasn't top-notch."

Stacie lifted a brow. "We'll see." She set down her fork and, leaning back in her chair, she considered Julia through narrowed lashes. "I suppose you've heard the rumors. Large sums of money are missing and now the books aren't balancing. Jerry Fein is pulling out his hair — what's left of it, anyway."

Julia nodded. She'd heard. Of course, it was only speculation.

Stacie leaned forward. "But I still don't think we need a consultant, rather a new accountant. Consultants downsize. Now it's middle management that'll most likely get cut — and that's you and me, Juli!"

Julia didn't reply, but she had heard a similar rendition of the state of Weakland Management's affairs from Ken Driscoll, one of the Portfolio Managers.

Looking at her wristwatch now, Julia made her excuses to Stacie. "Your computer program awaits — gotta go."

"By all means," Stacie retorted. "Oh, and let me know what you think of Mr. BC."

Julia frowned, puzzled. "Mr. BC?"

"Business Consultant."

With a thumbs-up sign and a wink, Julia nodded. "Got it. Code names, right?"

Stacie laughed. "Right."

Smiling, Julia deposited her dishes on the conveyor belt in the kitchen area and then made her way toward the elevators.

Weakland Management was housed in a building three stories high. On the first floor were the locker rooms, Sir Walter's Restaurant, the mail room, and security office.

The second floor housed Customer Service, Data Processing, Information Systems and Public Relations.

Finally, on the third floor were the executive suites where Bill Weakland, his vice president, and all six of the portfolio managers worked. From their computer terminals, they kept track of the Dow Jones averages and, by phone, they bought and sold stocks and bonds all day long. The company's sole accountant, Jerry Fein, worked up there, too, and on some days the stress level was so incredibly high that no one in his right mind ventured farther than the second floor.

Julia reached her department by eight forty-five and had fifteen minutes in which to plan and organize her day. Her office, located in the back of the department, was tastefully decorated, though devoid of any personal items. Julia strived to keep her personal and professional life as separate as night and day. It was all part of the distance she had decided on so long ago. The fewer questions about Jesse the better.

At nine o'clock, Julia's employees began to stroll into the department. Angela Davis, her Assistant Manager, was the first to actually enter the office. She was short in height and on the heavy side, though she wasn't at all unattractive. She dressed well and had long, dark brown hair and large, mournful, brown eyes.

"These are for you," Angela announced with a smile as she set down a vase of white peonies on the glass-protected surface of Julia's desk. "First pick of the season."

Julia nearly groaned aloud. More peonies.

"You okay?" Angela asked, looking concerned. "I mean, you're not allergic to these things, are you?"

Julia forced a tight smile. "In a way, I guess I am. Would it be all right if we set the vase next to the coffeepot?"

"Oh, sure." Angela picked up the flowers and left the office. With a heavy heart, Julia watched her go, hating the fact that she'd never gotten over her feelings for Mark Henley. Every spring, memories of what she and Mark shared flooded back like April showers and they lasted until July! And then, of course, Jesse was a constant reminder.

24

"What, daydreaming already? It's only five after nine."

Julia looked over at her office door and smiled when she saw Ken Driscoll standing there. He was attractive almost pretty actually, with his light brown hair, big green eyes, and slim physique. Ken was most definitely on his way up the corporate ladder. He talked of little else. His career meant everything to him and that was about all he and Julia had in common: their career goals.

"I worked all weekend," he was saying now. "What about you? Did you have a nice weekend also?"

Julia nodded. "I worked as well, but from home using my computer modem."

"Good for you. I tried to call you several times, but only got your answering machine." Ken paused, curiosity alighting his large, almond-shaped eyes. "You must have been out."

Julia nodded, remembering that she and Jesse had gone over to the Frenches' for dinner on Saturday evening.

Suddenly voices and laughter outside of Julia's office caused Ken to stand up a little straighter and wear a more serious expression.

"It's Bill," he said in hushed tones. "And

he's got his consultant with him. They're making the rounds this morning, meeting all the employees. I had my turn already." By the look on Ken's face, Julia surmised that Ken's territory had somehow been tread upon. She'd seen it before whenever macho ego clashed with macho ego — like two oncoming locomotives on the same track.

Bill poked his head into her office. "G'morning, Juli."

"Good morning." She pushed a smile onto her face.

"Do you have a minute to meet Weakland Management's new business consultant?"

"Of course." Julia knew the question was a mere formality. Bill expected she'd always have "a minute" at his request. He owned the place, after all.

The consultant stepped into the office, and Bill made quick introductions. "Mark, this is Juli, the Manger of IS ."

Her jaw fell slightly as she viewed the man before her. Sandy-blond hair, cropped short and worn carelessly, framed the handsome face of the man who haunted her dreams. Weakland Management's new business consultant was none other than Mark Henley!

Like an automatic gesture, he held out his hand. "Nice to meet you, J—"

He paused abruptly, his bright blue eyes now taking in every feature, every contour of her face. He smiled, looking rueful at first and then... delighted?

"Julia," he said, making her name sound like a caress, "it's... it's good to see you again..."

"You two know each other?" Ken asked at once.

Mark nodded, his eyes never leaving Julia's face. "We were... we went to high school together."

Julia felt the air returning to her lungs. Her heart, pounding before, was slowing to its normal pace; however, she couldn't think of one single intelligent thing to say. If she thought Mark Henley was handsome before, he was ten times more so now. His once youthful, ruddy complexion was now rugged and mature, but he possessed the same wolfish grin she always remembered.

And then it surprised her to realize just how angry she felt at seeing him again. Mark, standing here in her office. This was her office, her career, her new life since he'd left her standing in the chapel so long ago. How could this be happening?

Bill cleared his throat, looking suddenly

uncomfortable. "Yes, well, perhaps you two can get reacquainted over lunch."

"It's a date," Mark said with that charming smile of his. And before Julia could tell him that she never took a lunch, he and Bill were gone.

Turning back to her desk, Julia never saw the scowl on Ken Driscoll's face. In fact, she had forgotten all about him!

Chapter 2

"So who is Mark Henley to you, anyway?" Ken asked for the second time.

"What? Oh, I'm sorry, Ken. what did you say?"

"How do you know him? Our new business consultant?"

Julia shrugged her shoulders in what she hoped was a flippant manner. "Mark is just some guy from high school. That's all."

"That didn't seem like 'all'." Ken searched her face until Julia turned away.

"Ken, I have work to do ."

"Of course I guess I just want to know that Henley isn't anything more than a friend."

After he left, Julia began to fret. She thought of Jesse, and a little chill passed through her as she imagined Mark discovering that he had a son. She knew she should tell him before he heard it from somebody else. Would he be angry? Would he feel cheated out of fatherhood or would he want nothing to do with either of them? The latter was what Julia feared most. Jesse would be devastated to learn he had a father and then feel the sting of his father's rejection. Julia simply couldn't let that happen.

Julia somehow worked her way through the morning. She managed to push aside her tumultuous feelings for Mark until noontime arrived and so did Mark.

"Are you ready for lunch?" he asked, walking into her office with a galling air of confidence.

"I didn't get a chance to tell you," Julia replied coolly, "but I generally work straight through."

"Okay. No problem." But instead of leaving, Mark walked farther into her office and shut the door.

From behind her desk, Julia stood, her heart hammering once more. "What do you think you're doing?"

Mark smiled, though it didn't quite reach his eyes this time. It was a sad looking smile. "It's good to see you, Juli," he said softly.

She produced a curt smile. "I wish I could say the same, but I can't."

"I can accept that."

"Good. Now, if you'll excuse me, I have work to do."

Mark, however, didn't make a move. "For years I pictured you happily married with a pack of kids somewhere."

"Well, if you remember, that was the original plan."

"Touché, Juli."

She closed her eyes against an enormous wave of pain. "Please, Mark . . ."

"All right. I'll go."

He moved toward the door, then paused, his hand resting on the doorknob. "I've been trying to track you down for years, Juli." He turned around to face her. It was all she could do to hold her emotions in check. "It seemed you had disappeared off the face of the earth, but I never gave up hope in all my searching."

"You can't possibly expect me to believe that."

Mark shrugged. "It's the truth, although you're obviously not ready to hear it yet. But someday, Juli, I'm going to tell you all of it."

She forced a smile. "I would be happy to talk to you as one professional to another, but that's where I draw the line. Now, if you'll excuse me—"

"But I need to tell you, Juli. I must."

31

Mark paused once more, this time raking a troubled hand through his hair. "And for both our sakes, you're going to listen."

With that, he walked out of the office, leaving Julia fuming over the threat.

"I've been a wreck all day," Julia admitted as she and Barb sat on the wide front porch of the Frenches' home. Jesse and his "Uncle Glen" were away on errands. "I couldn't concentrate on anything."

"Oh, I imagine you had quite a shock today, honey," Barb replied. She was a short, jolly woman with a sweet disposition and, though she had never born any children, she was as motherly as they came, and Julia loved her.

"What am I going to do, Barb? It's Mark. I never thought I'd see him again. And what about Jesse? I've managed to forestall him every time he's asked about his father. But do I tell him now or do I wait and talk to Mark first?"

Barb clucked her tongue. "You're in a pickle, all right."

"I'll say. And can you believe that Mark had the audacity to say he's been trying to track me down for years? What a lie!"

"Are you sure it's a lie?"

32

"Of course I'm sure." Julia shifted uncomfortably then. "No, I take that back. Barb, I'm not sure of anything right now."

"Well, let's think about this for a moment." She paused, doing just that. Then she met Julia's stare. "I remember when you first moved in with us. You told me how hurt you were when Mark left you on your wedding day. And then to discover Jesse was on the way . . . you didn't know how things were going to turn out."

Julia nodded sadly. It had been a very bad time in her life.

"But what did you do then? What brought about a change?"

"I turned to God," Julia replied easily. "You know that. You're the one who led me to Christ."

"And you've still got Him, Julia," Barb said with an affectionate smile. A gentle breeze wrapped around them. Strands of her strawberry blond hair threatened to come loose from the chignon she wore. "He's only a prayer away."

At Barb's reply, something tugged on Julia's heartstrings. When was the last time she'd gone to the Lord with a problem? Too long, she supposed. But there was a time when she conversed with God on a daily basis. When had it stopped? Julia didn't know. However, one thing seemed certain —if she ever needed God back in her life, now was the time.

On Wednesday evening, Bill Weakland invited his employees to a business dinner at the country club. It was an annual company event, occurring every June, and various topics of interest were discussed. Typically Bill led the meetings, although he was known to invite guest speakers or elect different department heads to the podium. Tonight, Mark was scheduled to speak.

Parking her car, Julia entered the club and headed for the reserved banquet room. As she neared the doorway, she spotted Mark and her step almost faltered. She lifted a determined chin and marched straight ahead, refusing to let him intimidate her and despising the fact that he did anyway.

For the past two days, Julia hadn't seen much of Mark since Bill Weakland occupied most of his time. And that was just fine with her. The less she saw of him, the less he could affect her. However, tonight he stood, greeting employees as they entered the banquet room, and there was no way Julia could avoid him.

Mark nodded politely. "Good evening, Juli."

"Good evening," she replied coolly. But then she turned and smiled a greeting at Bill.

"Juli, you're prompt as always," he said. "You'll be sitting at my table tonight."

"Thank you, Bill."

Then, without a glance in Mark's direction, Julia set out to find her assigned table. Off-white linen tablecloths covered their surfaces and matching napkins had been carefully laid at each place.

Julia sat down and greeted some of her co-workers. They were all from various departments. It was Bill's effort at forcing acquaintances and, as Julia listened to one of the women talk about the woes of dictation, she glanced curiously at the name card on her right side. Ken Driscoll. And, on the left . . .

Julia groaned inwardly. Of course. It would have to be Mark Henley.

Dear God, she silently prayed, *I've been asking You what to do for two days, and I've been reading my Bible, but I'm just as confused as before. And now this.*

Stacie Rollins suddenly showed up and took her assigned place across the table from Julia. "Well, well," she crooned, "isn't

35

this just the sweetest little setup."

Setup is right, Julia thought, wondering if Mark had anything to do with the seating arrangements tonight.

Stacie cleared her throat. "Will you be going to the Brewer's baseball game on Friday the twenty-first, Juli? It's a company event, really, and the tickets are inexpensive."

Julia shook her head. "Maybe next time." She had taken that very afternoon off since her parents were coming to pick up Jesse and take him up north for a week. She didn't use much of her vacation time, but somehow it had all worked out for which she was thankful.

Bill was suddenly standing at the podium. "I'd like everyone to take their places," he announced. "Our food will be coming shortly."

Minutes later, dinner was served — grilled pepper steak, sautéd vegetables and rice pilaf. Normally Julia would have enjoyed the expertly prepared food; however, with Mark sitting beside her, she had to choke down every bite.

"So tell us about yourself, Mark," Stacie ventured. "Where did you acquire your education?"

"UCLA."

Surprised, Julia glanced over at him. She had assumed that he stayed in Oregon all these years, finished college and then worked with his father. Questions filled her heart as Mark caught her eye and smiled.

"Are you a home-grown California boy?"

He chuckled at Stacie's question. "No, actually I'm from the Midwest."

Julia's heart began to hammer. *Don't say it Mark,* she pleaded inwardly.

But he did. "In fact, Juli and I grew up together in Lyon, Illinois."

"Is that so?" Stacie drawled, giving her a speculative glance.

"I think we met on the playground," Mark replied, "when Juli was in Mrs. Craig's first grade class."

"You remember her name?" Julia asked incredulously.

Light laughter frittered around the table.

Mark nodded. "I remember a lot things," he said, looking directly at Julia. His expressive blue eyes darkened with emotion and the underlying meaning of his words rang in her heart, fostering an unbidden hope . . . which annoyed her to no end!

How can this man incite all these different feelings in me at the same time? Julia wondered.

Bruce Johnson, from the Public Relations Department, began asking Mark some more questions about his education. As Mark replied, Julia discovered he had earned his Bachelors and Masters degrees, both in Business Management.

"And he's working on his Doctorate," Bill interjected. "Just needs to finish up that old dissertation." He gave Mark a friendly slap on the back. "Right?"

Mark grinned. "That's right."

"Mark comes highly recommended from a good friend of mine," Bill added. "I've got a world of confidence in him."

"Thanks, Bill." Mark suddenly looked a little embarrassed by all the fuss being made over him.

"Well, well, isn't that impressive," Ken said in a tone that made Julia wonder ~~it~~ sounded sarcastic at best.

The conversation shifted to hobbies. Mark liked boating, golfing, biking and he loved hiking in the mountains. Suddenly Julia wished she could go home. She didn't want to know what Mark loved.

"My very favorite hobby, though," he admitted sheepishly, "is working on cars."

Julia brought her head up quickly, and Mark met her gaze.

"It was Juli's dad who taught me every

thing I know ___ and that's how I worked my way through college. Working on cars, rebuilding engines."

Julia swallowed hard, and it took everything in her to tear her gaze from his. Then, in an attempt to hide her discomfort, she looked at her wristwatch. She wished Bill would begin the meeting.

Someone changed the subject and suddenly separate conversations ensued around the table. Julia caught snippets, but wasn't really listening carefully to anything particular.

That's when Mark nudged her. "Help me with something, will you, Juli?"

She gave him a suspicious look. "That depends."

He smiled at the tart reply. "Listen, I'm a Christian and . . . well, I've been looking around . . . can you suggest a good church for me around here?"

Julia pulled her chin back in surprise. "A . . . church? For you?"

Now it was Mark's turn to look surprised. But then his expression changed to apparent regret. "Is that really so hard to believe, Juli? That I'm a Christian man now?"

She shrugged, deciding to answer his first question and ignore his last. "There's a Bible-believing church right up the road from Weakland Management. It's the one I belong to."

Just as soon as those final six words tumbled out of her mouth, Julia could have bit off her tongue. The last thing she wanted was for Mark to show up at church and invade her faith as well as her life. However, she couldn't retract the offer now with any semblance of dignity.

A slow smile began to spread across his face. "Are you a believer, too?"

She nodded.

"That's great — really great. When did it happen for you?"

Julia took a long, pensive drink of her mineral water. She didn't think it would hurt to tell him. "About eleven years ago."

"Happened for me about six years back." Mark paused. "Were you praying for me, Juli?"

The question momentarily threw her. Praying for him? Why, she'd done nothing but rue the day she'd ever met him — except, of course, where Jesse was concerned.

Fortunately for her, Julia never had to reply. Bill began the business meeting and the dinner dishes were quickly cleared.

"Thank you all for attending tonight," Bill stated. "As you're aware, we have a new business consultant and he'll be reporting directly to me. Some of you may already know that Dave Larkey, our Vice President, resigned."

Gasps of surprise echoed around the room while Julia and Stacie exchanged curious glances. Julia, herself, had had no idea that Dave resigned and, by the expression on Stacie's face, it appeared she hadn't known about it either.

"That's only one of the many changes that'll occur," Bill continued. "Mark has been hired to reorganize and restructure Weakland Management, so I'd like him to stand and say a few words."

Gliding his chair back, Mark stood and walked to the podium where he began a very eloquent presentation, complete with an outline that was handed to every employee.

"If you turn to page five," Mark was saying, "you'll see my itinerary. For the remainder of this week and all of next week, I'll be working closely with Bill, learning more about the company as a whole. Then, I'll be spending one week with each department, evaluating its efficiency. I'll report my findings to Bill and then we'll reorganize accordingly."

He's likely to be here till Christmas! Julia

realized with dismay. She had been half hoping that Mark's stay would be very temporary.

Julia sighed. Then, looking back at the outline, she noticed that Mark planned to start with Customer Service. Her department was third on his list, but Julia was fretting already. It had nothing to do with her department, per se; she ran a tight ship. Everything was in order. No, Julia's fretting came straight from her heart.

"Inevitably," Mark continued, "there will be changes, just as Bill mentioned, so I'm counting on everyone's cooperation. Cooperation, in fact, will be essential to my work and for the good of the company."

The meeting ended at nine o'clock sharp and, while the employees with questions gathered around Mark and Bill, everyone else went home. Julia was part of the latter crowd.

"So, what did you think?" Stacie asked as they walked to their cars.

Julia smiled. "About the meeting? Or Mr. BC?"

"Why, Mr. BC. Who else?"

Julia laughed. "Well, I think —." She paused. Actually, Julia didn't know what to think. Finally, she said, "He puts on a fine presentation."

Stacie lifted a brow. "I asked your opinion on him, not his presentation. I mean a girl would have to be in a coma not to notice the man. He's gorgeous! And the looks he was sending you."

Julia felt her face warming red, and she wondered if her flaming cheeks matched this evening's earlier sunset.

"Well, in any case," Stacie said, "it's just too bad that he's married."

"Married? Who?"

Stacie turned to give Julia an exasperated frown. "Mr. BC, that's who."

"Mark?"

"Come on, Juli, didn't you see the wedding ring on his left hand? I mean, really, that's the first thing I look for, and he's wearing one."

"I didn't notice."

Stacie shrugged. "Well, here's my car. I'll see you at work tomorrow."

As she watched Stacie drive away, Julia's heart plummeted. She tried to convince herself that she was glad Mark was married because now she could harden her heart against him and not feel guilty about it. Furthermore, she told herself that Mark didn't deserve to know about Jesse; he wasn't worthy of the title "Father."

However, Julia Rose McGowan had lied

to herself before, some twelve years ago, and she knew the sting of consequence. She had to face the cold, hard facts: Mark was married —. and he still had to be told about Jesse.

Chapter 3

The following morning dawned cold and rainy; however Julia decided to take her habitual run in spite of the weather. It was a challenge, too, considering that she'd tossed and turned for most of the night. She'd been so tired and yet she hadn't been able to fall asleep — not with the words "Mark" and "married" hammering away at her subconscious.

I don't care, Julia told herself for the umpteenth time as she jogged her last quarter of a mile, heading for home. She was soaked to the skin and the rain kept falling, but to Julia it felt refreshing. The cold rain did wonders for her swollen eyes and tear-streaked cheeks. Memories, like ugly demons, continued to surface, and Julia couldn't seem to steer her mind clear of them. Mark. She had loved him so much. Mark. He had been her best friend ... even better than her girlfriend Kathy. They had talked and dreamed together, planned their future together . . .

So what? That was twelve years ago. I don't care if Mark is married! Julia declared inwardly as she entered the condo. *I've got my own life. I've got my work . . . and Jesse.* Julia was only too glad that her son hadn't witnessed her fitful night since he stayed over at the Frenches' because of the meeting at the country club.

In the back hallway, Julia began to peel off her soaked wind-suit. Then she pulled on her bathrobe, which she had strategically laid over the kitchen chair. She swallowed down a painful lump and willed herself not to shed another, single tear. What had she expected? How absurd it was to think that Mark would have stayed faithful to her memory all these years when he couldn't even show up at the church to fulfill his promises! And yet, Julia had stayed faithful to Mark's memory . . . except, she had to admit, it hadn't totally been by choice. She simply had never met another man to whom she was willing to give her heart.

That's because Mark stole it, the rat!

She showered, and more memories assailed her then. This time, memories of Jesse. He had been a good-natured baby, one who didn't mind being left for college

46

classes and part-time jobs. Then he grew into a good-natured boy. It had taken Julia six years to earn her Bachelors Degree, after which she'd obtained the Information Systems position at Weakland Management. She didn't know what she would have done without the love and support of Barb and Glen. They nurtured her through her pregnancy, and they loved Jesse almost as immediately as Julia had. Then they had helped raise him.

Julia's parents, too, had been a great source of encouragement and, over the years, they became close friends with the Frenches. So, with her family cheering her on, Julia worked her way through college, determined to make something of herself.

Feeling that same self-determination growing inside of her, Julia dressed for work. She dried her eyes and carefully applied her makeup. Then, just as she was on her way out the door, she saw her Bible on the coffee table. *My devotions. I didn't have them this morning.* She really didn't feel like having them this morning, either; however, her heart seemed to prod her onward, toward the coffee table.

The devotional book and her Bible in hand, Julia took in the daily reading and then followed up with the coinciding passage from Matthew 11:28–30. "Come unto me all ye that labour and are heavy laden, and I will give you rest. Take my yoke upon you, and learn of me; for I am meek and lowly in heart: and ye shall find rest unto your souls. For my yoke is easy, and my burden is light."

Those words were like a soothing salve to Julia's heart. Her emotions were in such a tangled mess that she did, indeed, feel "heavy laden." She needed that "rest" that Jesus promised. Why had Mark reappeared in her life after all these years? Why did he say that he had been trying to "track her down" when he was married? He had promised to love her forever, except he married someone else! The realization of it hurt terribly, yet she knew she had to be honest with herself and at least admit that, yes, it hurt.

Picking herself up, Julia gathered her attaché case and purse. She was pensive as she left her apartment and drove to work. Part of her felt spiritually uplifted because of her devotions, yet Jesus seemed very far away. Where was He in all of this? Didn't He care that she was miserable?

Walking into Weakland Management, Julia met up with Angela Davis. "Everything all right, Juli?" she asked, trying to

48

pull her from her meditative mood. "Our handsome new business consultant doesn't have you worried, does he?"

"Yes, he does," Julia replied tightly, as they walked through the locker room. "But not in the way you think."

Angela seemed to ponder the remark momentarily. "I heard you guys grew up together," she commented, walking beside Julia as they headed for Sir Walter's Restaurant.

"We did."

"So this situation is like too close for comfort, huh?"

Julia forced a smile. "Yeah, something like that."

"Well, as always, if there's anything I can do to help, let me know."

"Thanks, Angela. As always, I appreciate your offer."

Julia surveyed the food and then selected her breakfast a warm, flaky croissant and a sliver of Brie cheese. Angela had fruit salad, served in the shell of half a cantaloupe. Together they sat down near the windows and began to eat.

"Good morning, Juli Angela."

Julia managed a smile. "Good morning, Ken."

"Mind if I join you lovely ladies?"

49

Without waiting for a reply, Ken pulled out a chair and sat down. "These waffles are my favorite! And I absolutely must eat them with an indulgent serving of Sir Walter's famous strawberry syrup."

Sitting across from Ken, Angela shook her head. "How come men can enjoy their 'indulgent servings' but we women pay for ours in inches to our hips?"

Julia grinned.

"Now, listen here," Ken replied with a slight smile curving his pretty-boy, handsome face, "I like a woman with a little meat on her bones. Indulge away, Angela."

"Not a chance," she retorted. "I've worked hard to take off that last twenty pounds. No indulging for me!"

"Such a pity." Ken sent a wink to Julia. "And how about you?"

"I indulge on the weekends only."

"Really?" Ken suddenly looked very interested. "What do you indulge in?"

"Chocolate *anything*." Julia couldn't hold back a soft chuckle.

Ken was smiling warmly at her now, and Julia grew uneasy. She could tell he was interested in her romantically and thought she should say something to discourage him. However, she figured Ken would lose interest in her as soon as he found out about Jesse. It had happened before, an interested man who lost interest as soon as he found out there was a child attached to her. Fortunately, Julia was never too heartbroken about it. She hadn't been the one interested, after all.

Glancing at her wristwatch then, she said, "You'll have to excuse us, Ken, but Angela and I are going to be late for work if we don't get going."

Nodding, he waved the ladies off while enjoying a mouthful of strawberry-saturated waffles.

"What do you think of him?" Angela asked, walking beside Julia as they headed for their department. "I'm just curious."

"Ken?" Julia smiled. "Oh, he's very dedicated."

"So are you," Angela observed.

Julia agreed. "I guess we have that much in common."

"Are you thinking of .+. dating Ken?"

"No," Julia replied, shaking her head. "I never liked the idea of dating my co-workers."

"Even if they beg and plead and turn on the charm?" Angela's chuckle had a cynical ring. "Juli, how could you resist? I don't think I could."

"Resist Ken?" Julia shrugged. "It's easy

for me here at work. My career is very important to me. In fact, it's more important to me than dating a begging and pleading co-worker, okay?"

Chuckling together, Julia and Angela rounded the corner. Then, entering the department, they met Mark who was obviously on his way out. In fact, all three of them nearly collided in the doorway.

" 'Mornin', Juli," he said good-naturedly. Looking at Angela, he said, "Good morning to you, too."

Angela looked suddenly uncomfortable, but mumbled a greeting before scurrying off to her desk. Julia just folded her arms tightly across her chest and lifted her chin. She was determined not to let her personal feelings affect her professional stance.

"Can I help you with something, Mark?"

He nodded, still wearing a charming smile. "I need a PC hooked up. Bill wants me to have access to every program you've got up and running. I have an office now upstairs. It used to be the small conference room." He paused, his gaze roaming over her in a quick head-to-toe motion, his expression saying he liked what he saw. "So what do you think?"

I think your wife ought to know about the looks you're sending me, Julia fumed. However she replied, "I have to iron out some kinks in Customer Service's new program this morning, but I'll have your PC installed this afternoon."

"Good enough."

Julia gave him a dismissive nod and then made her way to her office. But, as she unlocked the door, she discovered that Mark was right on her heels.

"How 'bout dinner tonight?" he asked, entering the office behind her. He closed the door, much to Julia's aggravation. "I'll pick you up about seven o'clock. Just give me your address and phone number."

"You've got to be kidding!" She glared at him with arms akimbo.

A puzzled brow marred Mark's handsome face. "What do you mean? Of course I'm not kidding." He paused, looking thoughtful. "I figured we broke the ice last night at the business meeting. It seemed like we did, anyway."

Julia fairly gaped at him. *He's married and he's asking me out. What a jerk!*

"Look, Juli," Mark said softly, seriously, "there's a lot you and I have to talk about. There's so much unsettled between us and I . . . well, I need to see it settled."

Julia narrowed her gaze suspiciously. "Okay, let me get this straight. You're asking me out for the sole purpose of seeing things settled between us. Correct?"

Mark seemed to weigh her words before nodding. "Correct. Look, Juli, you're a part of my life that I've never been able to resolve, and I can sense that it's the same for you, too."

He smiled, his blue eyes softening, and Julia knew he was determined to get his way. Some things never changed!

"Come on, Juli, what do you say? Dinner tonight. It's perfectly harmless. I promise."

Julia rolled her eyes. "Yeah, sure, I've heard your promises before."

Mark seemed to grow suddenly very serious. "Juli, that's why we need things settled between us. I owe you an explanation and an apology and I {.. well, I desperately need your forgiveness."

The way in which Mark said that caused Julia to wonder if he was having marital problems, and all because of their past. Then she wondered if it was really her responsibility to help Mark lay it to rest.

"Juli," he asked softly, "what do you say? Let's talk over dinner tonight."

"I'll think about it," she replied, turning away from him and sorting through some mail on her desk. She hoped she sounded bored and distracted even though she was anything but.

"Well, that's all I ask," Mark said, "just that you think about it."

With that he left her office, leaving Julia alone with her tumultuous thoughts.

Chapter 4

It wasn't until two o'clock that Julia found enough time and resolve to hook up Mark's PC. She wheeled the color monitor, hard drive, and keyboard to the elevator on a cart. As she entered his office upstairs, Mark stood immediately and helped her unload the equipment. Julia was both surprised and impressed when Mark began plugging the PC components together with their proper cables.

And then a flash of silver from his left hand. So, it's true.

Julia's heart felt like it was going down for the last time and, in an effort to save it, she forced herself to concentrate on the business at hand.

"I'm going to program your PC into a community printer that's located near the portfolio managers," she told Mark.

"That's fine."

"And I downloaded everything from my PC to yours, but only because Bill requested it. I'm not pleased about it at all."

"Why's that?" Mark asked with a slow smile that was so charming it caused Julia to bristle all the more.

But, to him, she merely replied, "It gives me an uneasy feeling to know that other co-workers make that consultants have access to my programs. It's kind of like too many cooks in the kitchen. The more people entering into the Program Manager files, the more potential there is for error."

"And I agree," Mark said, still smiling. "I promise I won't mess up your computer programs, Juli."

Another promise.

Taking a slow, deep breath then, Julia determined not to let Mark get to her anymore. She needed to put aside her personal feelings. After all, this was the work place, and she had a job to do.

Julia cleared her throat. "If you'd like to pull up a chair, Mark," she offered in the politest tone she could muster, "I'll give you a briefing of the system."

He nodded and pushed a chair in beside her; however, with him so close, Julia could scarcely concentrate. She could smell his cologne, like leather and spice, and there was an aura about Mark that commanded respect, not in a military sense, but in a professional one. Yet he was quick to smile, seemed eager to be friendly, and he had an athlete's look about him.

Jesse would like him, she thought, wondering simultaneously what in the world she was ever going to do.

"Juli?" Mark gave her a nudge with his elbow. "Wake up, lady!" he said, grinning.

Julia shifted in her chair, feeling embarrassed. "I'm sorry. I was thinking about something else."

"That's okay." He chuckled softly. "Now what about this new program that you wrote for Customer Service? Tell me about it. Show me how it works."

"All right." Julia signed onto the program and showed Mark the basics as she gave him an overview.

"I see." Mark seemed thoughtful. "Weakland Management is certainly a rapidly growing company."

With a nod, Julia smiled inwardly. She felt quite pleased with her accomplishment. She rather thought that Mark looked impressed, too. And wait until she unveiled her new software ideas for the portfolio managers. Ken had been a big help to her in that regard, during the early stages of her program's development.

Mark suddenly reached over with his left hand and pointed to the computer screen. "So this is where the callers' names and addresses go, huh?"

"Right."

As Julia looked at the monitor, she couldn't help but look at Mark's wedding ring. It was, after all, right there in front of her nose. And when she focused on it and not what Mark was pointing at, a vague sense of familiarity arose in her until at last it took hold of her recollection. *That's our ring!* she realized. *The one Mark bought for our wedding . . . it had belonged to a set . . .*

"Juli, honestly, are you with me or not?"

In reply she stood up abruptly, sending the wheeled chair rolling backwards. "You're despicable!"

"Excuse me?" Mark stood as well, arching questioning brows.

"You heard me, you lowlife snake in the grass!"

Mark brought his chin back at the insult. "Juli, what in the world ——?"

"In fact, you're lower than a snake. You're a worm!"

"Julia," Mark's voice beheld a hint of warning, but she ignored it.

"Bad enough that you're married and sending me suggestive glances, but that you couldn't even buy yourself a different wedding set ⊥. that's inexcusable, unforgivable ⊥. and just plain old bad taste!"

Mark turned on his heel and headed for the door. Julia fully expected him to storm out of the office or, at least, slam the door, but Mark did neither. He simply closed it softly and then walked back over to where she stood, still smoldering.

Sitting on the corner of his desk, one leg dangling over the side, Mark gave her an earnest look. "I'm not married, Juli," he said. "Never was."

She folded her arms across her chest and lifted a defiant chin. "Yeah, that's what they all say."

Mark grinned. "All of them?"

Julia gave him a leveled look. "A figure of speech, Mark."

His grin broadened, and Julia realized that he was teasing her ⟋ and it hurt. Tears threatened in the backs of her eyes, but Julia willed them away.

"Mark," she began in voice that sounded broken to her own ears, "that was our wedding set. How could you flaunt it in front of me? How could you flaunt it in front of everyone here at Weakland Management? My co-workers think you're married now. In fact, it was Stacie Rollins who pointed out your ... our ... wedding ring, and ..."

"And she's probably a good example of why I'm wearing it, too!" Mark interjected. "At least a good example of one of the reasons I'm wearing it."

Puzzled, Julia could only stare back at him.

"I put this ring on," Mark explained gently, "after my first consulting job. I was a novice, and I didn't want anything to make that, anyone distracting me from my work. Besides, I wasn't interested in a romantic relationship, and I figured wearing a wedding ring would forestall any predatory females," he said emphatically. "It usually works, too."

Julia stood there, wondering whether to believe him.

"I'm not married, Juli," Mark said, in a low, sincere tone of voice. Then he took her hand. "I wouldn't purposely hurt you ... not again. I can tell that you're still hurting over what happened twelve years ago."

Julia fought the urge to yank her hand away, except that would only prove his point.

"Besides," he added, "how could I ever marry someone else when I could never forget you? Which brings me to the other

61

reason I'm wearing this ring."

This time she did pull her hand away. "I don't want to hear it. You were always such a sweet talker. I can still see you sweet talking poor Miss Lamont in English class. I don't think you ever had to write an English paper."

This time Mark laughed, nodding. He obviously remembered, too. "All right, I'll admit that I was a sweet talker. But I sincerely meant what I just said about never being able to forget you."

She narrowed her gaze suspiciously.

"Look, I have no dark, ulterior motives, I guarantee it. But I do think we need to talk. Tonight. Over dinner." Mark's voice was soft and persuasive. Standing, he guided her toward the door, placing his hand on the small of her back. His blue eyes shone with promise. "I'll pick you up at seven o'clock."

Before Julia could utter a single reply, Mark had ushered her out of his office. She decided to leave peaceably, since she didn't have much choice. She was in the hallway now, right across from the portfolio managers' workstations with Ken Driscoll staring holes right through her.

Julia gave him a quick smile. But then, walking toward the elevators, she realized that she hadn't given Mark her address. Turning, she walked back into his office.

"Forget something?" he asked.

"No, but you did," she replied tartly.

"And what's that?"

"My address."

Mark grinned mischievously. "Got it right here," he said, pointing to the computer screen. He turned the monitor so she could see it. "The personnel file. Too bad there's only demographic data on these things, though. I would have liked to have more information on each employee."

"Such as?" Julia ventured.

"Such as a resume—something to give me background info on everyone." Mark shrugged. "I suppose I'll have to hit the guys in Human Resources, huh?"

"You mean Public Relations."

"No, I mean Human Resources." He smiled lazily as he sat back in his swivel chair. "The first major change I'm going to suggest to Bill is that we create a Human Resources Department. Instead of the PR Department doing the hiring and keeping tabs on employees, Human Resources will do it. Bill can hire experts who know the State's labor laws. PR can't manage it any longer."

"I see," Julia said, feeling suddenly a

little concerned for her own position. What if Stacie was right? What if middle management was on its way out? But this was her career! Her life's blood! How would she and Jesse ever survive?

Just then, Mark looked up and smiled warmly. "I'm going to do a little playing on my new PC," he said sheepishly. "I'm a bit of an egghead, so don't worry." He lowered his voice then. "See you tonight, Juli. Okay?"

Still feeling troubled, she could only nod as she turned and left his office.

I can't believe I'm doing this, Julia thought as she changed from her three-piece suit of skirt, vest, and matching jacket, into a light-blue silk dress. *I can't believe I agreed to go out to dinner with Mark!*

Julia was only grateful that Barb had no reservations about keeping Jesse overnight for the second time this week. Jesse, too, hadn't seemed bothered when Julia spoke with him on the phone. He said his friend, Sam, was going to sleep over and that Uncle Glen was going to take them both fishing in the morning.

"Just don't forget that I'm taking a half-day off tomorrow because Grandpa and Grandma are coming to get you on their way to Minoqua."

"I can't wait!" Jesse had declared. Julia smiled, knowing how he loved to vacation with her parents up in northern Wisconsin.

"Well, Jess, I'll miss you," she said at last, "but it'll only be for a week. Then I'm on vacation, too, and I'll ride up with Aunt Barb and Uncle Glen."

"Are you going to stay the whole week, Mom?" Jesse had asked. "Or are you gonna have to go back to work early like usual?"

Julia had felt a stab of guilt at the questions, but determined to stay up north the whole week. Jesse was glad to hear it, too. With that, she told him she loved him and hung up the phone.

Vacation, she thought now as she brushed out her auburn hair, *the word does have a nice ring to it.* Unfortunately, the week after vacation would be her week with Mark, one on one in IS. Julia decided she couldn't think that far ahead. Dining with Mark tonight seemed foreboding enough.

He was prompt, ringing her front door-bell at precisely seven o'clock. Julia let him into the front hall of the apartment. Hers was a modern, bi-level unit with entrances leading directly outside.

"Come in," Julia invited. Then she reached for her raincoat hanging on the hook of the wooden coatrack.

"You look beautiful as always," Mark commented, helping her with her coat.

"Thanks," she murmured. Turning then, her gaze met Mark's and something warm and familiar passed through Julia. How natural it would be, she thought, to walk into his arms and feel his lips on mine. Her heart fairly skipped a beat at the mere thought of Mark's kiss. "Are you sure you're not married?" she asked weakly. She didn't want to be experiencing these emotions for someone else's husband.

Meanwhile, Mark was hooting at her question. "Juli, there are two things I'm certain about in this world, my salvation and that I'm not married." He laughed once more. "Let's go. I'm hungry."

She allowed him to take her hand as they walked outside to where Mark had parked his car on the street.

"This?" Julia asked when he was about to open the door for her. "This is your car?"

"She's a beauty, isn't she?"

Julia had to smile as she surveyed the light blue, two-door Chevy Impala. She would have thought Mark would be driving a sporty little red thing. But instead he drove a relic!

"My dad would love this car! What year is it?" she asked, climbing into the front seat.

"It's a '66," Mark replied, closing the door.

As he walked around to the other side of the car, Julia was amazed at how big the front seat was. Blue upholstery with vinyl trim, it seemed as large as her living room sofa!

"She was a wreck when I first bought her," Mark said, starting the engine. The car purred like a giant cat. "I rebuilt the engine, polished up the interior, which included replacing the old, torn vinyl seats with these. I found them at a junkyard. Then came the paint job. Now this baby's as good as new."

"My father would love this car," Julia repeated.

"You know, I thought about your dad a lot while I was fixing it up."

Julia didn't reply, knowing how her father felt about Mark.

"So where am I going?" Mark asked. "Where's a good restaurant around here?"

"There's a steak house right up Appleton Avenue."

"Let's give it a try."

They drove to the restaurant in foggy weather. After they arrived, the waitress led them to their table—a quiet corner booth with a rounded seat. Julia slid in on one side and Mark on the other. After they had ordered two coffees, the waitress left them to study their menus.

"So, tell me about yourself," Mark ventured. "Where did you go to college?"

"The University of Wisconsin, here in Milwaukee."

"Major?"

"Computer Science."

"I figured." Mark grabbed a warm bread stick out of the linen-covered basket which had been set on the table. "Bachelors? Masters?"

Julia paused. "Bachelors." She wondered if her position at Weakland Management would be jeopardized when Mark discovered that she didn't have as much education as some of the other managers.

He didn't, however, seem concerned about it for the time being. "Why did you leave Lyon?"

The question didn't surprise Julia in the least. In fact, she was ready for it. "I wanted to start a new life." She reached for a bread stick of her own.

"Kathy told me you were sick when you left."

Julia tore at the warm bread. "I was." The sickness Mark referred to had been due to her pregnancy. Kathy, of course, hadn't known about it. No one had. "I got better."

"That's good. Nothing serious, huh?"

Julia just shrugged.

"Can I tell you what happened to me after I left Lyon?" Mark asked. "I think after all these years you deserve an explanation."

Julia looked up from her plate. She really didn't want to talk about this. It was still much too painful.

"Please, Juli," Mark persisted, "let me offer up an explanation and an apology."

After a moment's thought, Julia nodded. She should, at least, allow him that much . . . shouldn't she?

Chapter 5

"I was a very confused young man when I arrived in Oregon," Mark began. "My parents were the mainstays in my life. When Dad left us, it shattered my security and my faith in people and relationships."

Julia nodded. She had guessed as much from Mark's last letter.

"So I ran away. That's really what it was," Mark admitted candidly. "I was scared, Juli. I knew I loved you, but I started feeling claustrophobic in Lyon. I thought my future looked like a dead-end street."

"Well, that's fine," Juli replied, trying to keep the edge out of her voice, "but it would have been nice if you had said something sooner than our wedding day. In fact, it would have been nice if you would have said something. But you left me with a a lousy letter and a church full of people!"

This isn't going to work, she decided, tossing her linen napkin onto the bread plate. She would have left the table, the restaurant, too, if the waitress hadn't shown up and blocked her way out of the booth. And she would have refused to place an order except Mark took the liberty of ordering "tonight's special" for the both of them.

"Juli, please, hear me out," he pleaded after the waitress walked away.

"I don't know if I can," she replied honestly. The twelve year ache in her heart had surfaced, and it hurt as much as if it had happened only yesterday.

Mark's expression softened as he moved closer to her. He put his arm around her shoulders while taking hold of her elbow with his other hand. It was like some gentle warning that she couldn't run from what he wanted to say to her tonight.

"I should have taken you with me," Mark whispered, causing tears to form in the backs of her eyes. "I just wasn't thinking straight at the time. But I tried to come back for you . . . later."

When Julia didn't reply, Mark continued his explanation. "I worked for my dad's company that first summer as I prepared to go to college in the fall. I wanted to contact you, Juli, but I was still running scared. When fall came, the company downsized and cut my dad's entire division. He decided, then, that he couldn't afford to pay my tuition, even though he had promised. I got angry and we had a terrible fight. It was then that my eyes were opened to how wrong my dad's lifestyle was and how wrong I had been to think every married man ended up like him. Within the week, I had moved in with a friend from work. When he went back to school at UCLA, I went with him. He was in his third year and he helped me get registered and apply for student loans.

"That's when I decided I wanted you with me, Juli," Mark told her, his mouth still close to her ear. "I wrote you letters, begging you to come to California and I tried to telephone on numerous occasions. Your father intercepted all my phone calls, and I imagined he did the same with my letters. So I tried to get to you through Kathy. That's when she said that you were sick all summer and left Lyon."

Julia just nodded, but she couldn't bring herself to tell Mark why. Not just yet. Not when she was feeling so vulnerable.

"I tried to find out why you left town and where you'd gone, but no one would say, and your father kept me away from your family."

"He was trying to protect me," Julia said in his defense. "My father knew how hurt I was and—"

"I know," Mark replied. "I know that now, and all I want is to make things right somehow."

A few moments of silence followed, and Julia took the opportunity to shrug out of Mark's hold and move away—but only slightly. On one hand she liked being close to him, remembering how much she once loved him—or, perhaps, she still did. But she couldn't think straight with his nearness.

"Throughout my college years, I tried to contact you. I wrote letters. I tried to call." Mark pursed his lips in the way Julia always remembered. He had a way of doing it, too, bringing his bottom lip out and up at the same time, which made him look stately and important. Mrs. Baker used to encourage Mark to use the gesture during debate class. She said he looked like a politician. "Have you ever been able to forget me, Julia?" he asked softly. "I've never been able to forget you."

Julia could only shake her head in reply. How could she tell Mark that every springtime he crept into her thoughts? How could she say that every time she looked at

Jesse, she was reminded of his father?

"As I told you," Mark began once more, "I became a Christian about six years ago. That changed my perspective on a lot of things, and it somehow made me more determined to find you."

Julia looked over at him, wondering if he really meant it. She couldn't think of why he'd lie, but she was afraid to believe him. She was afraid he'd hurt her again. However, his face, so close to hers, his charming ways and warm, endearing words, were more wonderful than anything she'd ever dreamed of.

"Then I ran into your brother Rick last summer," Mark explained. "It was at a camp in South Carolina. I was in Charleston on business and got invited to a revival meeting at this camp." Mark chuckled. "And what a surprise to learn that Rick is a youth pastor in Indiana. Unfortunately, he and his youth group had been at camp all week and were leaving the same night I arrived. I did, however, manage to talk to him for a little while. He's a fine man, Juli."

She nodded. She was very proud of both her brothers; however, she was now curious as to how much Rick had shared. Did Mark know about Jesse? And why didn't he let on if he knew?

"Rick told me that you were living in Menomonee Falls, Wisconsin. He couldn't remember the name of the company you worked for, but he told me you were doing something with computers. So I began to pray that the Lord would find me a consulting job in the area ┼Milwaukee, preferably, but I would have taken something in Chicago. Then things began to develop through a friend of a friend and, here I am." Mark laughed. "But, Juli, when I was praying, I only expected God to take me somewhere in the vicinity of where you were ┼not the same city or the same company. God most certainly does do exceedingly, abundantly above all we ask!"

"I guess He does," Julia replied skeptically. She wasn't at all convinced that Mark's being here was answered prayer. "What else did Rick say?" she couldn't help but ask then.

Mark only shrugged. "He said just about all he could say over a quick cup of coffee in the lodge. We didn't have much time together."

Julia felt pacified for the moment. She thought she'd like to verify Mark's story with Rick later.

A tossed salad was served and then

dinner arrived. As they ate, their conversation was light, Mark relaying stories of his "college days" at UCLA.

"I love California," he said. "Have you ever been there?"

Julia shook her head in reply. She couldn't bring herself to say that being a single parent took all her free time and most of her extra money. Even so, Julia knew she'd never have it any other way. She loved Jesse with a mother's fierce, protective love and, from the day he was born, Julia knew that he was a very special blessing.

"Did you know that my parents got back together?" Mark asked.

Julia nearly choked. "Back together?"

Mark nodded. "They've been together for the last eight or nine years now."

Julia raised astonished brows. "Your mother took him back? After what your father did to her?"

Mark nodded. "Incidentally, my parents are both believers now, too. They have been for years, although Mom has been a Christian since she was a teenager. I never knew that until after my own conversion to Christ. Mom said she had gotten away from the Lord for a while."

Julia felt amazed.

Finally they finished eating and left the restaurant. It was still drizzling outside, and there was a damp chill to the early summer air.

"I'll turn on the heater," Mark said, after they had climbed into his car.

"Thanks." She couldn't contain a shiver.

The ride back to Julia's apartment was quiet, save for the mellow pianist playing on the car stereo. After parking in front of the apartment complex, Mark leaned over and shut off the music.

"So, what do you think?" he asked.

"What do I think about what?"

"About what I said tonight."

Julia shrugged. "I don't know what to think, Mark, and that's the truth."

He nodded. "I suppose I should give you time to sort everything out. Here," he said, reaching across her lap and opening the glove compartment, "I want to give you my phone number just in case you need to get a hold of me after work."

He scribbled down his number. When he handed the slip of paper to Julia, she stuffed it into her purse.

"Thanks. And thanks for dinner tonight," she said, reaching for the handle. She opened the car door and climbed out. Mark did the same and met her on the sidewalk. It was obvious that he meant to walk her to the front door which sent Julia's heart beating wildly. Would he kiss her good night? Would she be able to stand it if he did? What if her knees gave out right there on the front walk? What if he wanted to come in ——?

But Mark surprised her on all accounts. "G'night, Juli," he whispered, placing a firm, but gentle kiss on her cheek. "See you tomorrow."

She nodded, feeling somehow disappointed. Then, as if he sensed it, Mark said, "I know what your kisses are like, Juli-bean. They're like those potato chips advertised on TV —— I could never have just one."

Julia managed an embarrassed grin. Even with all the years between them, Mark could still read her so well. "Good night," she said at last.

He waved and Julia watched him walk back to his car, marveling at this side of Mark she'd never seen before. Years ago, he would have taken what he wanted despite the consequences, be it potato chips, a kiss, or much, much more.

Inside her apartment, Julia changed into her most comfortable clothes. Then she plopped herself on the sofa, reflecting on the entire evening. She glanced at the telephone and picked it up, impulsively dialing Rick's number. Julia had a good relationship with her younger brother, in spite of the gap in their ages. She knew he'd understand the reason for her call. She knew Rick would listen and then answer in all honesty. And she just had to know for sure . . .

"Sorry, I know it's late," Julia said when her brother answered, sounding sleepy.

"That's okay, Juli," Rick replied. "What's up?"

She paused. "I had dinner with Mark Henley tonight."

"Oh, yeah?" There was a smile in Rick's voice. "You two kiss and make up?"

"No. I guess Mark is too much of a gentleman for kissing."

"What?"

Julia chuckled. "Never mind." Again, she paused. "Mark said he saw you last summer, Rick, is that true?"

"Yep. We had a nice talk, hasty as it was. I answered every question Mark asked me, too. I just decided I wasn't going to lie anymore. You really need to talk to him about Jesse, Juli. You know, in many situations, keeping silent is the same as lying in my book. Jesse has been a secret for too long.

79

It's only right that Jesse be allowed to know about his dad."

"I know——." Julia was momentarily pensive, feeling the burden of her responsibility. Telling Mark and Jesse about each other wasn't going to be easy, yet she knew she had to do it. But for now, she was preoccupied with questioning Rick and, for the next few minutes, he confirmed everything Mark had said as truth.

Finally, he added, "I think our family needs to practice some forgiveness, and I think all dark secrets need to see the light of truth for a change. That's my opinion, Juli ——my two cents worth."

After a moment's pause, Julia replied, "I appreciate your straightforwardness, Rick. I'll consider what you've said."

Julia said her good-byes and then hung up the phone. Feeling a myriad of emotions, she made herself a cup of herbal tea. Back in the living room, Julia telephoned her mother, inquiring over the letters Mark claimed to have written.

"It's true, dear," Caroline said. "Mark wrote to you on numerous occasions. I . . . I saved the letters."

"You did?" Julia was actually quite glad about that. She thought she'd like to read them.

"It wasn't my place to throw them away, Juli," her mother said. "Your father would have insisted, though ⊥ . if he had known about them. Perhaps I was wrong in keeping them a secret, but . . . I just didn't think it was right to throw your mail in the garbage."

"Mom," Julia asked softly, "will you bring the letters with you tomorrow when you come for Jesse? I've got the whole afternoon off ⊥ . I guess I'd like to read them."

"Of course. I've got them in a stationary box. I'll pack them in my suitcase."

"Thanks."

"You're welcome. Now tell me how your dinner with Mark went."

Julia had to smile as she recounted the evening. "And he didn't even kiss me good-night, Mom," she concluded. "Well, he did, if you call a little peck on the cheek a kiss. He's different. I'm beginning to see that."

"We all make mistakes, Juli," Caroline said.

"I know."

"I think it's time we forgive one another." Caroline paused. "And in that regard, please continue to pray for your father, Juli. I've thought for years that the

81

bitterness in his heart against Mark — and the whole Henley family — has been in the way of his accepting Christ."

"Really?" Julia hadn't ever thought of something getting "in the way" of her father's salvation.

She promised to keep praying, and then they made some last-minute plans regarding the trip up north. Finally Julia hung up the phone and prepared for bed. Crawling beneath her sheets and thick down comforter, she listened to the rain as it splashed against her bedroom windows.

She replayed the two telephone conversations in her mind. The words "bitterness" and "forgiveness" seemed to pluck a sad cord in Julia's heart. Had she, like her father, been harboring a bitter spirit all these years? Perhaps without realizing it? Had she only thought that she forgave Mark?

"Of course I forgave him," she muttered, turning into her pillow. "I'm a Christian."

Suddenly Julia recalled her conversation with Mark last Wednesday night at the business dinner. "Were you praying for me, Juli?" he had asked. *No, I never prayed for him,* she had to answer in all honesty.

Many pensive moments ticked by, and Julia had to finally admit it — she had

82

never forgiven Mark. And, though she loved Jesse with her entire being, he had been a constant reminder of the pain Mark inflicted upon her when he left her so long ago.

She had never forgiven Mark for that.

"Oh, Lord," she breathed into the darkness of her bedroom, "I want to forgive Mark. Help me forgive him."

Then, moments later, she knew what she had to do.

Julia threw off the bed covers and walked into the living room. Grabbing her purse, she fished through it until she found the slip of paper with Mark's phone number. Then she picked up the telephone and dialed.

"Mark . . . ?"

He paused. "Juli? Is something wrong? What is it?"

She had to smile at the sound of concern in his voice. "Nothing's wrong . . . I just have to tell you something. You know how, as Christians, we're not to let the sun go down on our anger?"

"Yes."

"Well, I've been letting the sun go down on my anger for twelve years."

Mark didn't reply.

"And I haven't been acting like much of

83

a Christian this week, either," Julia admitted. "It was . . . well, it was such a shock to see you again."

"I understand. You know, I always planned to telephone you first, once I finally found you." He chuckled. "Sorry, but I never got the chance."

Julia smiled in spite of herself.

"Well, I'm sorry, Mark," she finally managed to say. She marveled at saying it, too. Last week if anyone would have told her that she'd be apologizing to Mark Henley, she would have laughed her head off! However, her behavior of late warranted an apology. There were times this week when she'd been downright rude to Mark.

"I forgive you," he said easily. "No problem."

"And . . . and I forgive you, too, Mark," she said, softly, earnestly. She swallowed a sudden painful lump. But instead of willing it away, she chose to deal with it. "It hurt so badly," she confessed, "and sometimes it still hurts . . ."

"Juli, I'm so sorry." Mark's voice was soft, as if it somehow hurt him, too.

"Apology accepted."

There was a smile in his tone when he said, "Juli, those words are music to my ears."

"I'm glad. Well, good night."

"Good night, Juli," Mark replied. "Sweet dreams."

As Julia put the receiver in its cradle, she felt as though a load had been taken off her shoulders. She realized, then, that unforgiveness was a heavy load to tow. Now that it was gone, however, Julia felt the joy of the Lord returning to her heart. *So that's why He seemed so far away. With so much bitterness in my heart, there hadn't been room for Jesus!*

Crawling back into bed, she knew that there were a great many things still unsettled between herself and Mark. But, at least she seemed to be headed in the right direction now.

Chapter 6

"G'morning, Juli," Mark said jovially as they met in the hallway at work the next morning. "Lovely weather we're having."

Julia smiled a greeting, but rolled her eyes. There was a torrential downpour outside, the skies were gloomy and gray ... but, sure, it was "lovely weather." Then Mark walked right into her, sending the memos in her hand flying. His right arm circled her waist as he pretended to be surprised. Julia immediately recalled how Mark used to do this to her in high school. It had started by accident but quickly turned into one of those silly games that sweethearts played.

"You nut!" she cried, laughingly. She noticed, however, that Mark's arm around her felt firm and secure. Then his gaze met hers and for a long moment she was reminded of the love she'd seen shining from his blue eyes so many times. Could it be? There again . . . ?

Suddenly uncomfortable and confused, Julia stepped out of his embrace and stooped to pick up the colored memos. Mark joined her, chuckling. "You're just lucky no one was around to see that!"

"Why do you think I did it?" He chuckled again. "Really, I couldn't help it, Juli," he admitted. "I saw you coming and the temptation was just too overwhelming."

Smiling, Julia shook her head at him.

"Need some help?"

Looking up, she saw Ken Driscoll standing over her. "No, I'm all right. Thanks." She hoped he couldn't see her cheeks warming pink over the less-than-professional incident that had just occurred.

"Guess I've got to watch where I'm going," Mark said with a sheepish grin.

They stole an amused glance at each other, and Julia had to bite the inside of her lip in an effort not to smile.

At last the memos were collected and Julia and Mark stood at the same time. "Here, I might as well give you one of these now," she said, handing a memo to Mark. "It'll save me a trip up to your office."

"What is it?"

"Print-outs of the week's stock market

activity," Ken replied. "All employees receive one every Friday morning. I'll take one, too, Julia. Thank you." He scanned it and then looked back at Mark. "Of course, this is just a briefing."

Mark nodded, looking over the memo in his hand. "Thanks for the info, Ken," he said politely. Then to Julia, he smirked and said, "Nice running into you."

Julia didn't reply except to give Mark a pointed stare since Ken was still standing beside her and obviously had no intentions of moving until she did.

"I see you and our business consultant are getting along better," he commented lazily as they walked toward Customer Service. "And, come to think of it, I don't believe I've heard you actually laugh out loud the entire six months I've worked here."

Julia paused. "You mean you heard me just now?"

"All the way down the hallway."

Julia grimaced.

"Angela told me you were quite stressed out for a few days, so I'm glad to see you've overcome whatever was bothering you."

Julia smiled. "Yes, I did." Then she quickly changed the subject. "Will you take these upstairs for me?" She counted out several memos.

"What do I look like, the mail boy?" But Ken took the memos anyway and headed for his office. Julia walked into Stacie Rollins' department.

"Good morning."

Stacie sighed, looking harried. "Listen, Juli, if I can't figure out this new computer program by Monday, my goose is cooked . . . and so is yours!"

Julia set down the memos. "What's the problem?"

"This thing won't let me sign on, that's what's the problem."

Patiently, Julia took a chair and began to manipulate the keyboard while Stacie paced in frustration.

Julia smiled. "Okay, you're in. And I think you'll find that, once you get used to it, this application will be easier than the old one. Maneuvering the mouse will be easier and faster than using the keyboard."

"Yeah, sure it is," Stacie replied on a facetious note. "I had just better be able to impress Mr. BC with my looks, because I certainly won't impress him with my computer skills."

"Mark knows it's a new program," Julia replied, getting up from the chair so Stacie could take her rightful place. "I'm sure he'll be understanding."

Stacie lifted a brow. "You're singing a different song this morning, Juli. Yesterday you were wailing about having to let Mr. BC in on all your computer secrets." She tipped her head slightly. "What gives?"

Julia shrugged. How could she possibly explain?

"He's married, Juli," Stacie sang on a note of warning.

Again, Julia didn't know how to reply. She didn't have Mark's permission to say that he wasn't married.

"And aren't you one of those born-again people?" Stacie charged with a toss of her blond head. "I thought you told me you were "born again" that time your kid was selling tickets to some band concert at his Christian school. Doesn't the Bible say something about not getting involved with married men?"

"Yes and yes," Julia replied honestly to both questions. She found it interesting that even an unbeliever knew born again Christians were Bible-believing people and that one of God's commandments warned against committing adultery. Julia understood that she had a testimony to uphold. "You're right, Stacie, because of my faith I

90

would never enter into a relationship with a married man."

Stacie turned away with a little shrug of satisfaction and, as Julia made her way back to Information Systems, she knew she needed to be careful. As long as it was assumed that Mark was married, she had to distance herself. On the other hand, she had to get close enough to tell Mark about Jesse — and before he heard it from someone else.

"Jesse? Are you ready to go?"

"Yep!"

Julia grinned broadly as her son came out of his bedroom, pulling behind him the largest suitcase she owned. "Are you sure you've packed enough stuff?"

"I got everything."

"I'll bet you do," she said with a little chuckle. Julia looked at her parents, sitting at her dining room table enjoying a cup of coffee. "I think he's ready."

Roy McGowan stood and stretched. "Tell me again, when are you driving up?"

"Next Friday," Julia replied, "after work. I'll ride up with Barb and Glen."

He nodded in satisfaction. "And what's going on with that Henley kid?"

Julia and her mother exchanged glances

over Jesse's blond head.

"He's hardly a 'kid' anymore, Dad . . . and we'll talk about him some other time." Julia looked at Jesse then back at her father. "All right?"

Roy nodded. "Come on, Jess," he said, "you can help me repack the car. Why on earth your grandmother needed me to pull her suitcase out of the car, I'll never know."

"Thank you, Roy," Caroline said with a sweet smile to end his complaints. Then, once he and Jesse were out of the room, she added, "The box of letters from Mark is on your dresser." She paused, looking thoughtful. "I'm going to tell your father about them and how I saved them for you. I think he'll be angry, but I feel so dishonest. I shouldn't have kept them from you either, but I knew you wouldn't accept them."

"You're right. I wouldn't have even a week ago."

Julia grinned. "Tell Dad, and I'll talk to him, too, when I get up north next week. Between the two of us, we ought to be able to soften his heart."

Caroline laughed. "It's always worked that way before, hasn't it?"

Nodding, Julia smiled and hooked arms

with her mother as they walked outside. Her father and Jesse were already in the car and waiting to go.

Caroline kissed her cheek. "Good-bye, sweetie," she said, "see you next week."

"Okay," Julia replied, watching her mother climb into the car. "Bye, Jesse. I love you."

"Love you, too, Mom," the boy called from the backseat.

Julia stepped back as the car pulled away from the curb and waved as it disappeared down the street. With misty eyes at her son's departure, Julia watched the vehicle until it was swallowed in the fog and gloom. Then she ran back to her apartment and set the tea kettle to boiling. There was a chill in the air today and dampness had a way of seeping into her joints. This weather belonged to March or early April. Hardly appropriate for the end of June. Julia shivered.

Then she remembered the letters.

With eager steps she walked to the bedroom and picked up the stationery box from where her mother had set it on the dresser. It wasn't a small 6 x 9 inch stationery box, as Julia had presumed, but a 10 x 12 inch box that had obviously held business-size envelopes. Opening the lid,

Julia counted and quickly guessed that there were at least one hundred letters in the box. All addressed to her, all from Mark.

With a cup of tea in one hand, the box of Mark's letters in the other, Julia made herself comfortable on the couch and began reading. She was amazed that her mother had kept them in order. All the envelopes were still sealed.

Dear Juli,

I'm taking a chance in writing to you. I don't know if your father will even let you get this letter, but it's worth a shot.

I love you, Juli. I can't live without you. I should have never left you behind. We belong together. Soul mates, remember? That's what we always said

Julia groaned. This wasn't going to be easy. How did she ever come to believe that she could read Mark's letters the way she read computer programming material — emotionally unaffected? It was impossible. By the fourth letter, Julia was in tears. By the tenth she'd decided she couldn't read any further, and she had ninety more to go!

She cried and amazingly it felt good. She

allowed it, the crying, the cleansing. How long had she swallowed these tears? How long had she stuffed her feelings so far and deep inside herself, willing them never to surface? For years and years, she admitted inwardly.

With renewed resolve, she picked up letter number eleven. It was dated November 4, 1986. Mark wrote about school, his distant relationship with his father and some friends he met.

Juli, please come. You would love California. I've got a small apartment, but it's big enough for the two of us. We'll get married . . .

Promises, promises. No, this wasn't going to be easy. Christmas cards, birthday and Valentine's Day cards. "I love you, Juli," Mark had written inside them.

More letters. "Please answer me. I made a mistake and I'm sorry. I only hope your dad won't intercept this letter. He hates me, but I don't care. Until you say to my face that we're through, I'm going to keep on loving you . . ."

As the dates on the letters progressed, they gave testimony to Mark's education. He began using longer, more complicated words and sentences. Then, instead of handwritten, his letters were done on a typewriter or computer. However, they always said the same thing. "I love you." "I miss you." "I'm sorry."

Then Mark wrote about his conversion to Christ. The peace in his heart, the freedom in the Lord's forgiveness. Several letters later, Mark shared the Gospel and stated he was praying for her salvation. Little did he know, that she had been saved by grace nearly six years before he had.

Then Mark wrote about "Roberta" and Julia's heartbeat quickened. She read the letter anxiously, as though she were reading the latest, best-selling thriller.

I met someone. She's a Christian . . . but I need to settle things between us before I can begin a relationship with her. You must have received at least one of my letters — your lack of response indicates your disinterest in rekindling anything we might have shared in the past . . .

A series of letters followed. Three in six weeks' time. Mark stated that he had tried to telephone her, only to have her father answer. He tried to explain himself, but Roy McGowan wouldn't hear a word of it.

Mark phoned a few more times before the phone number was changed to an unpublished one.

Julia remembered when that had happened. Her father said it was due to "prank" phone calls. And here, all along, it had been Mark trying to reach her.

There was a wide gap in the letters, then. No more came for over a year. The next, a Christmas card, was signed very formally, "Love, Mark." But not "Love, Mark and Roberta."

The rest of the letters had come in the form of cards, Christmas, birthday; however, there were no Valentine's Day cards. No more words of love. No more pleas for their reunion. Then the frequency of his letters slowed dramatically until they all but stopped. Mark's last Christmas card came a year and a half ago, and there hadn't been anything since.

So whatever happened to Roberta? Julia knew it was none of her business, and she told herself she shouldn't care . . . but she did. And that was her biggest problem: she still cared for Mark. Very deeply. However, along with the admission came the fear of being hurt again. She could still feel the pain and devastation of his leaving and the horror of discovering she was expecting a baby. Julia didn't think she could ever live through his rejection again.

And so, with guarded heart, she folded up the last of Mark's letters and put it into the stationery box. She then carried the box into her room and set it on the top shelf of her closet. It fit among her shoe and hat boxes. It blended right in and soon she'd forget it was even there. At least she hoped she'd forget. However, it looked like Mark Henley was back in her life to stay, and what was she ever going to do about that?

Chapter 7

Julia pulled on her favorite denim skirt completing her Saturday attire. She wore a light-blue, scoop-neck T-shirt with long sleeves, light-blue stockings and her most comfortable denim slip-ons. Walking from her bedroom, Julia paused in the living room and picked up last night's newspaper from the coffee table. Then she searched for the time the art festival on the Lakefront began. Ten o'clock. *Good, I'll have plenty of time to get there.*

Julia enjoyed arts-and-crafts shows. She had dabbled with the idea of being an "artist" someday. She liked to draw and paint; however she knew she wasn't good enough to make any kind of living at it. As Barb had told her while she was in college, "You don't often hear of starving computer programmers, but you hear of starving artists all the time!"

Smiling at the recollection, Julia made a small breakfast and poured herself a cup of coffee. In her sunny yellow kitchen, she read her daily devotion and its Scriptural application. It helped ease her insecurities. She now felt prepared to face the day.

Julia rose from her place at the small table and cleared her dishes. After rinsing them, she grabbed her dry-cleaning and the garbage while she juggled her purse and left the apartment by way of the back door. With her hands full, however, she only managed to knock over the aluminum garbage can as she struggled with the lid.

"Want some help?" a male voice called from behind her.

Julia swung around and met Mark's smiling face. "What are you doing here?" she asked, surprised.

He shrugged. "I was ringing your front bell when I heard the garbage can ensemble here. I had a feeling it might be you."

"It's me, all right. I guess I took on more of a load than I could carry." Gratefully, Julia accepted his help with the garbage, noticing his attire. He wore a red, plaid, cotton shirt with a band collar and beige twill pants.

Mark turned and smiled. "Got plans?"

Julia nodded. "I'm on my way to an art festival."

"Want some company?"

She didn't, of course; however, the way he was looking at her reminded her of Jesse. *It's the eyes,* she decided, *and that Henley smile is irresistible.*

"Sure, come on along," she finally conceded.

Mark's smile broadened. "Where are we going?"

"I told you. It's an art festival."

"Yeah, but where?"

Julia stopped short on the narrow walkway between hers and the apartment building next door and laughed aloud. If Jesse wasn't his father's son! Mark's last question sounded like something that would have come right out of Jesse's mouth.

How will I ever contend with the two of them? Julia wondered, smiling at Mark.

"What's so funny?" he asked.

"Can I tell you later?" Julia lost some of her smile. "Seriously, Mark, there's something I need to tell you."

"Okay."

His blue eyes seemed to grow soft with compassion, an expression that belonged to this "new" Mark standing before her. It was all Julia could do to keep from blurting out her twelve-year-long secret— Jesse.

"Just don't tell me you're romantically involved with Ken Driscoll," he said, sounding like the Mark she remembered, "or I'll ⨉"

"Or you'll what?" Julia demanded, shocked by his response.

He smiled, but his eyes lost all compassion, and suddenly he was that hard-line business consultant who intimidated Julia to no end. "I'll tell Bill to fire him."

"You wouldn't!"

Mark chuckled while Julia momentarily chewed on her lower lip. She couldn't say for sure what Mark would do. In the end, she merely shrugged. "Well, no matter," she replied, "I am not romantically involved with Ken."

"Good," Mark said in a way that made Julia wonder if he'd been teasing her all along. After all, he probably didn't have the authority to tell Bill to fire anybody. Now, suggesting that he eliminate middle management . . . well, that could be different.

Wearing his prized wolfish grin, he took Julia's dry-cleaning from her as they continued to walk toward the front of the apartment complex. "I'll drive," Mark offered. "You can navigate since I'm new in town."

"Sure." Julia felt a little uneasy. It bothered her that she couldn't tell when Mark was teasing. "Hey, Mark," she asked suddenly before climbing into the car, "how did you pick up on Ken and me? I mean, there's nothing to pick up on, really . . . except that . . . well, I've suspected that Ken is interested in me."

"It wasn't too hard. He follows you around like a puppy. And I caught him hanging around your department at least ten times last week. Most times you weren't there, though. And once, Juli, he was in your office."

"In my office? What on earth was he doing in there?"

"Snooping, maybe. I don't know. Perhaps you ought to start locking your door when you leave your office."

"I can't. My employees need to get to the file cabinets and program manuals."

"Then maybe you ought to give one of them a spare key," Mark suggested. His eyes suddenly twinkled with mischief. "Now get in the car and we're not going to talk about work anymore today. Got it?"

"Got it," Julia replied on a note of resignation. Then she sighed. This wasn't exactly how she had planned to spend her Saturday.

Lake Michigan stretched eastward as far as the eye could see, a body of blue trimmed with whitecaps that lay beyond the park where artists had set up their work. The grass was soggy underfoot since yesterday's rain had saturated everything. Today, however, the weather looked promising. Partly sunny skies and warm breezes.

Julia and Mark walked through the rows of sketches and paintings, marveling at many and pondering over a few.

"What do you think it is?" Mark asked softly.

"It is very abstract, isn't it?" Julia replied, tipping her head from one side to the other. "A seascape, maybe."

"Seascape? How do you see that? Looks like a scrapyard."

"Oh, hush," Julia admonished him on a teasing note. "You never had an eye for art. What do you know?"

"I know that's not art, okay?"

Julia chuckled under her breath and moved on. She had to admit, Mark could be fun company. It had been a long time since she felt comfortable enough around someone to joke and laugh. Her best friends were Barb and Glen French, despite their age differences. While the Frenches were looking forward to retirement, Julia's career had really just begun.

Mid afternoon, Julia and Mark finally

stopped for lunch. Purchasing hotdogs and nachos from a vendor they wandered closer to the lake and found a vacant picnic table.

"Very pretty area," Mark commented, his gaze scanning the lakefront.

Julia agreed. "It's a very popular area, too. And look that way, Mark, to the south of here is where all the ethnic festivals are held. Polish Fest, Irish Fest, German Fest, African World Festival and Indian Summer. But the biggest festival is called Summerfest. It's usually too rowdy for my liking."

Mark nodded, seeming to be content at letting Julia babble.

"I like the State Fair." She caught herself before adding that it was Jesse's favorite, too. She took a bite of her hotdog instead.

Mark had finished his in two bites. "How are your folks, Juli?" he asked, changing the subject.

"Just fine. Enjoying their retirement."

"Good. Mine, too."

A moment passed. Then another. Finally, Julia decided to tell him about the stationery box in her chest. "My mother saved all your letters," she said, hoping she wasn't dropping an ugly bomb on this perfectly lovely afternoon. Then, again, "the bomb" was going to come sooner or later.

Mark narrowed his gaze. "Saved them? My letters?"

Julia nodded. "She didn't feel right about throwing them away and, for that reason, she kept them from my father."

Mark shook his head, looking rueful. "It's a shame your mother didn't do more than just save my letters, Juli. I wish she would have given them to you."

"No, Mark. Back then, I would have never accepted them. I would have most likely torn them to shreds without even opening them. I was determined to forget my past, which included you . . . us. I wanted to start a whole new life."

"And it seems as if you have."

"Yes, I have."

"Are you happy, Juli?"

"Of course I am," she replied a little too quickly. "I stay busy . . . my work is very important to me."

"So I've gathered. In fact, it seems you have a whole different set of values . . . to go along with your new life, I mean . . . since I knew you last."

The crowd from the art festival had diminished and, except for some brave sea gulls loitering around the picnic table. She and Mark were free to hold a private conversation without anyone else overhearing.

"I'm not the same person you left behind in Lyon," Julia told him.

"And I'm not the same person who left you."

"I can tell from your letters." She smiled at his shocked expression. "Mom and Dad have a cabin in Minoqua," Julia explained, "and they stopped yesterday on their way up. Now that they're retired, they spend their entire summers up north and don't go back to Lyon until about October.

"Anyway, I asked Mom to bring me your letters and she did." Julia looked up from where she had been picking at a tortilla chip and met Mark's intent gaze with one of her own. "I read them last night. Every one."

"And?"

"And, I believe you. I mean I believe that you told me the truth on Thursday night."

Mark looked momentarily hurt. "Did you think I'd lie?"

"I don't know. Forgiving you and believing you are two very different things. I forgave you last Thursday night, but I wasn't sure I believed you."

"And now?"

"Now I know you told me the truth."

Again, the awkward silence. Julia thought

of how ironic it was that nature could be so noisy at a time like this. Lake Michigan's rushing waves slapped the shoreline and the sea gulls, circling above, gawked at each other, paying no heed to the intensity of their conversation.

Finally, Julia couldn't stand it any longer. "Can I ask you something personal, Mark?"

"Sure," he said easily.

"It's really none of my business."

"Ask away."

Julia paused. "Who's Roberta? I mean, I understand who she was . . . well, that you were interested in her. I guess I'm wondering what happened."

Mark gave her a gentle smile. "We dated for about a year, but when it came time to make a decision about marriage, I didn't have any peace about it. Our relationship came to an end because I couldn't promise her a future. I wasn't convinced that Roberta was the woman God had chosen for me."

"Hmmm . . ." Julia was momentarily pensive. Then suddenly she sensed that now was the time. She had Mark's undivided attention. They were talking about the hurtful past . . .

"Mark, I've got to tell you something.

Maybe I should have told you sooner," she said quickly so she couldn't change her mind. "Perhaps I should have told you years ago, but the truth is, I never thought I'd see you again. I really believed you didn't want anything to do with me."

"Not true."

"Yes, well, I know that now. And this whole thing seems more and more like a Shakespearean tragedy."

Mark grinned slightly. "Tell me, Juli. What's on your mind?"

"Well, when I left Lyon, I wasn't just sick, Mark. Oh, I was heartsick and depressed, and my parents were worried, but when I became physically ill, they took me to old Doc Kramer. That's when I learned that I — I was pregnant."

Julia looked down at the cheap paper plate in front of her. She was afraid of what she'd see in Mark's expressive blue eyes. Disappointment? Disdain? Both?

"I kept the baby," she continued, "even though my parents and I had planned to give him up for adoption. But I couldn't do it. The very moment I looked into his little face, I knew he was mine — ours, and I loved him immediately. Giving him away would have been like cutting my very heart out."

Finally, Julia felt brave enough to chance it. She lifted her gaze and, much to her wonder, she saw tears pooling in Mark's eyes. The sight was enough to make her cry, too, since the Mark Henley she had known back in high school would have rather died than let anyone see him shed a tear.

"Please, go on, Juli," he said, blinking back his emotion.

She nodded. "His name is Jesse, and he's a terrific kid. He knows the Lord, wants to do right, and he favors you in looks."

For a long, long time, Mark said nothing. He just sat there with his elbows on the picnic table, his hands folded tightly in front of him, his mouth resting on his knuckles. Finally, he said, "I always thought that was it, Juli, the reason you left Lyon. Your brother only confirmed it. You see, I've known about Jesse for almost a year."

Julia was stunned. "Rick? He told you?" At Mark's nod, she felt betrayed by her own brother. But then she recalled him saying, *I answered every question Mark asked me. Jesse has been a secret for too long.*

"Yes, he told me. And, Juli, you can't begin to imagine how many times I wanted to see you and our son, once I found out where you were. I nearly went crazy all these months. But I wanted the timing to be right. Perfect. And I wanted God to direct my every step. I knew how hurt you were, and still are, to some extent."

Julia's jaw dropped. "You knew? You knew all this time?" Angry now, she grabbed her purse and rose from the picnic table. "You could have said something, instead of playing games, Mark. I've been a nervous wreck ever since you came to town, wondering how on earth I'd explain that you have a child. Here you knew all along!"

"Juli, I only wanted you to trust me enough to tell me yourself."

"Trust has nothing to do with it. It's called honesty!"

Suddenly Julia wondered over Mark's motives for showing up in Menomonee Falls. What if the only thing Mark wanted to settle between them was custody of their son?

"Juli."

But it was too late. She turned and ran toward the bustling Lincoln Memorial Drive. It wasn't long, however, before she realized how futile her attempt at escape really was. She had come here in Mark's car!

Minutes later, he caught up and fell into step beside her on the sidewalk.

"Juli, would you stop? Can we talk about this like two mature adults?"

"Don't worry," she shot at him, "I have no intention of denying you your parental rights."

"I'm not worried. Come on, Juli, we were getting along so well."

She slowed her pace, but only to move aside and let a young man on roller blades whiz by.

"Come on, Juli, let's keep up the dialogue," Mark said. Several minutes passed as they kept walking. "Look, there's a bench over there in the shade. Let's sit down."

By now Julia had worked out some of her frustration, and she realized she was going to have to talk with Mark sooner or later.

With a reluctant nod, she followed Mark across the street and walked beside him through the park toward the brown, wooden bench. It was near one of the park's steep ravines and with the buds of spring all around them, they sat down.

Mark stretched his right arm across the top of the bench behind Julia, while she folded hers tightly across her chest.

Finally, Mark asked, "What's his middle name? Jesse's?"

"It's Mark. After you . | ."

He smiled. "Well, thanks for that. It tells me a lot."

Mark's arm suddenly moved from the bench to her shoulders. Julia's first impulse was to shrug it off, but she couldn't deny the comfort of his touch.

"Jesse Mark — McGowan, huh?"

Julia nodded.

"I'd like to change that. I mean, I'd like my son to have my last name."

She fretted over her lower lip. "He doesn't know about you, yet. I've got to tell him."

"When?"

"He's up north with my parents."

"When will you tell him, Juli?" Mark's tone was insistent.

"I don't know. Don't pressure me. I'll tell him as soon as I can."

Mark shook his head. "Not good enough."

Julia turned, looking at him in all her surprise. "What do you mean, 'not good enough'?"

His eyes bore into hers. "I'm not waiting another twelve years to meet my son."

"He's eleven," Julia stated sarcastically.

"And you wouldn't have had to wait at all if you would have shown up at the church twelve years ago like you were supposed to!"

Mark ignored the reply. "You've got ten days, Juli. After that, I'll tell Jesse myself."

She glared at him. "Don't you dare threaten me."

Mark smiled charmingly. "Juli, I wouldn't threaten you. That's a promise."

"Well, what a relief," she said with a bitter laugh. "For a minute there, I was worried. But you, Mark, make empty promises, so I guess I have nothing to fear."

Standing, Julia slipped the strap of her purse over her shoulder and turned and walked away. "I'll tell Jesse when I think the time is right. . and I'll take a cab home."

Mark let her go.

Chapter 8

Julia sipped her herbal tea while the incessant pounding at her front door continued. She knew it was Mark, but she refused to open her door. However, she was softening, minute by minute. The pounding had been going on for ten minutes now. What would her neighbors think?

"All right, all right, I'm coming," she called at last. Walking to the front door, she slipped back the chain and unlocked the door.

"You are one stubborn woman!" Mark declared once she opened it.

"Whatever."

Mark narrowed his gaze. "Did you ever stop to think about anyone else through all of this, Juli? Did you ever think that maybe I was hurt, too? Well, I was. and I still am. I've missed so much of my son's life Jesse's first smile, his first baby steps . throwing a football with him . Little League Baseball. And my parents . did you ever think of them? My mother loved you like a daughter ⨍ she's always felt bad over what happened. But that you never thought to let her in on Jesse's arrival, it broke her heart. My dad's, too."

"For your information, Mark," Julia said, hands on hips, "I purposely didn't tell your mother because I didn't want to add to her shame and suffering. She was already contending with what happened between her and your dad. You're the one, Mark, who doesn't think of anyone else but yourself!"

He leaned against the doorframe, looking weary. "Listen, I didn't come here to argue with you, believe it or not. I really just wanted to make sure you got home all right." He paused. "Good night, Juli."

As he turned and walked away, something caught in her heart. A shred of sympathy for the man. Perhaps it had been his admission of hurt feelings or maybe it was his remorse over all the years he'd missed with Jesse. In any case, Julia didn't want to let him go away like this.

"Mark?"

He paused at the end of her walkway and turned a questioning gaze in her direction.

Julia stepped out of her front entrance and walked to where he stood, leaving the door behind her wide open. "I know it's hardly compensation for everything that's happened," she began, "but ─┼─ . well, maybe we could call a truce and you could join me for supper tonight at Barb and Glen's. I'm sure they'd like to meet you. They're like my second parents, and they were a great support to me after I left Lyon. They're aware of the situation, Mark, but I can guarantee they'll remain objective. On the other hand, Barb's a great cook, and I've got stacks of photo albums full of Jesse's baby pictures. I could bring them along ─┼─ ."

She held her breath, awaiting Mark's reply. She felt foolish for propositioning him like this, and yet, for some crazy reason, she hoped he'd accept the offer.

He did. "I'd like that, Juli," he said softly.

She smiled. "I'll get my things and we can go."

"Oh, look! This picture was taken at the Milwaukee Country Zoo," Barb said, sitting beside Mark, explaining each snapshot of Jesse's life. "There's this little train that goes around the zoo, and Jesse just had to ride on it. In fact, we used to take him for a ride on the train first thing just so he wouldn't beg the entire time we were trying to see the animals."

117

Sitting across from them, Julia smiled and stifled a yawn. They were on the fifth photo album and Barb was still going strong.

"Jesse loved trains. He still does, doesn't he, Glen?"

Her husband nodded quietly from where he sat in the other armchair.

"Oh, and this picture was taken at a family reunion that same summer . . ."

Julia smiled though she was struggling to keep her eyes open. She sensed it was a losing battle and, next thing she knew, Glen was gently shaking her awake.

"It's after midnight, Juli," he was saying, "and Mark is leaving."

She roused herself and then pulled her stiff body out of the cushioned armchair. "Sorry to be such bad company," she told Mark. "I didn't mean to fall asleep."

"That's all right." There was a light in Mark's eyes that was soft and genuine.

Julia smiled back at him.

"I told Mark you'd be staying over," Barb was saying. "You might as well."

Julia nodded. She had extra clothes here and frequently spent the night, especially when Jesse was home and they all had plans for the weekend.

"I'll see you tomorrow, Juli," Mark said,

surprising her by taking her into his arms. He hugged her, kissing the side of her head.

"Good night, Mark," she replied, giving him a little hug and telling herself that this embrace meant nothing; it was just something from one friend to another. Her heart, however, seemed to beat contrary to that notion.

"And Mrs. French," Mark said, having released Julia, "I thank you for a wonderful meal. Best I've had since Christmas when I was home." Taking her hand, he patted it affectionately. "The meal was almost as wonderful as the company. Thanks for sharing your memories with me."

"Oh, my pleasure," Barb replied, blushing profusely. Her rosy cheeks spread to the tips of her ears.

Julia grinned. Mark Henley could charm the birds right out of the trees!

"And Mr. French, it was good meeting you."

"Same here."

Then after a firm handshake, Mark left.

"He's coming to church tomorrow," Glen told Julia, closing the front door.

Barb nodded in delight. "What a nice young man," she crooned.

Julia nodded for lack of a better reply.

Mark could turn on the charm when he wanted to, although, she had to admit that tonight had been extremely enjoyable.

Yawning, Julia walked down the hallway to the spare bedroom. Barb was right behind her and Glen stayed back to turn off all the lights.

"Good night, dear," Barb said in a motherly way as she kissed Julia's cheek. "You know, I'm experiencing a sense of peace over this situation. I've heard you speak about Mark through the years, and I know how much you've been hurt, honey, but I truly believe things are different now."

Julia had to agree; she'd seen the difference in Mark, too. "But I have to proceed with caution." If anyone understood her, it was Barb French. "As you're already aware, Mark is a consultant at Weakland Management for the next few months, and everyone thinks he's married since he insists on wearing that stupid wedding band!"

Barb's merry laugh rang through the hallway. "Oh, wasn't that the story, though? But I suppose there are unscrupulous women in this world who would like nothing better than to ruin a man's career, not to mention his Christian testimony."

Julia shrugged, too tired for further debates, especially where Mark was concerned.

Barb was standing beside her now. "I don't want you to think I'm taking sides, dear," she said, putting a large, comforting arm around Julia's shoulders, "but if you could have seen the way Mark looked at you while you were sleeping in that chair tonight, you wouldn't be so wary around him." Barb chuckled. "You did look awfully sweet, too, all curled up and sleeping peacefully. You looked like an angel."

Julia clucked her tongue in embarrassment.

"Glen saw it, too," Barb continued. "Mark couldn't take his eyes off of you."

"You're exaggerating."

"Why, I am not! In fact, I'd go so far as to say that Mark Henley is still in love with you!"

"All right, that's enough," Julia said lightly. "Time for bed. You're obviously delirious with exhaustion."

"Humpf!" Barb said, feigning indignation. She strode toward the bedroom door. "Suit yourself. Find out the hard way." She shook her finger at Julia then. "But I know love when I see it."

Julia rolled her eyes and saw her out. "G'night, Barb."

Closing the door, Julia turned and leaned against it. She had tried to cover her emotions in front of Barb; however, now that she was alone, there was no mistaking the tumult in her heart. *Mark still in love with me?* Julia shook her head disbelievingly. She didn't want to entertain such a thought because she feared it might grow into a precious, fragile dream that was sure to end up in pieces at her feet.

Not again, Lord, she pleaded. *Please protect me from getting hurt again.*

And with that simple prayer came the realization of just how dangerous a man Mark really was. He could take everything she held dear. Her career, her son — and her very heart!

✝ *Chapter 9*

"Did you have a good weekend, Juli?"

Standing in line at the restaurant, waiting for her turn to order with Sir Walter, Julia merely nodded. How could she tell Ken that she'd spent Saturday and Sunday with Weakland's business consultant? Very simply, she couldn't.

"I worked all weekend," Ken was saying.

Julia turned to look at him. "Did you get a lot done?"

Ken nodded, and Julia realized this last weekend was the first in many that she hadn't worked. And that little bit of time away had helped Julia see things differently ✝ in a healthier perspective, perhaps.

"Maybe some Sunday you could come to church with me, Ken," she impulsively offered. "There's a Bible study for single people, too."

"Not interested," Ken replied in a bored tone as he gazed over the food. "I'd rather work than go to church."

"Do you believe in God?"

"I believe in myself." Ken turned her way and his green eyes scanned her face. His expression was hard, even cruel — so much so, in fact, that Julia found herself taking a step back.

"I'm sorry, Ken. I shouldn't have put you on the spot that way."

He shrugged. Then, an instant later, his dark expression was gone. "God and church are not for me."

His simple reply somehow saddened Julia. However, when her turn came to order, she did so with fervor. Bacon, scrambled eggs and an English muffin. Normally she never ate this much in the morning, but for some odd reason she was hungry today. Perhaps it was due to the basketball game she and Mark had played in the rain last night.

Julia smiled inwardly, remembering. At ten o'clock, in the pouring rain with thunder rumbling in the distance, Mark had challenged her to a basketball game. Barb and Glen had laughed till their sides ached, watching from the dry, covered front porch. It was the stupidest thing she'd done in a long time, but it had been so much fun! And she'd nearly won the game, too, which came as no surprise to

Mark. He said he remembered how good she had been when she played on the girls' basketball team in high school. Now if only she didn't catch pneumonia .⟶

Julia chose a table near the windows and sat down. Despite the rain last night, the sun shone brightly this morning.

"I had hoped you would show up this weekend," Ken said, taking a seat on her right.

"Oh, well⟶I was , ⟶ busy."

At that precise moment, Mark appeared, a tray of food in his hands. "May I join you?" he asked, setting down his tray.

"By all means," Ken replied, though his countenance hinted at the contrary. He sat back lazily.

"Good morning, Juli."

"Good morning," she said with a smile.

"Say, Ken, I've been meaning to congratulate you," Mark said moments later. "I heard you acquired the Paxton account."

Ken's face immediately split into a huge grin. "I worked very hard on getting that account, thank you."

Mark chewed, swallowed, then pursed his lips thoughtfully. "It's a multi-million dollar deal, isn't it?"

"Sure is."

Julia considered each man as he spoke. She sensed that while Ken seemed proud and enthusiastic, Mark appeared to be troubled. She couldn't figure out why, until she suddenly remembered. The Paxton account ̶ wasn't that the one George Simmons, another portfolio manager, had been trying to secure? Julia was puzzled. What was Ken doing with the Paxton account?

"Nice people, the Paxtons," Ken was saying. "And they're very eager to invest."

"Great."

"I've given them several investment options and they're presently deciding on which is the most suitable."

"How did you hook them . . . the Paxtons, I mean?"

Julia suddenly felt as if she was watching a Ping-Pong match.

"Oh, I have my ways," Ken replied mysteriously. "However, I will say that I've got other irons in the fire."

Mark paused and looked up from his breakfast. "If you play with fire, Ken, you might get burned."

He laughed. "I think you've missed my point."

"Well, just so you don't miss mine, okay?"

Julia shifted uncomfortably. The atmosphere was suddenly laced with tension, and she debated whether she should excuse herself. But, then, she didn't have to. In a single, abrupt motion, Ken picked up his tray and left the table, making a racket as he deposited his dishes. Other employees in the restaurant looked over at Mark as if for an explanation. He offered none.

"Oh, boy," Julia muttered, nibbling on her bacon, "troubled waters ahead."

"And the boat's got a leak."

Julia frowned. "Ken?"

"I don't know," Mark replied. "I'm not sure what I'm dealing with quite yet."

Julia nodded for lack of a better response. Then she watched as Mark pushed around the food on his plate and for the first time since his arrival, Julia sensed the amount of pressure he was under at Weakland Management. *It can't be easy,* she mused, finishing the last of her breakfast. Mark had to insinuate himself into the company, knowing that some employees would be hostile to the changes he proposed. Julia had learned that that was why Dave Larkey resigned: he had been opposed to making changes.

Minutes later, they disposed of their

trays and dishes. Julia noticed that after the incident with Ken, Mark hadn't eaten much more. Her heart went out to him, which surprised her. The man was in a position to advise Bill to cut middle management, he could sue her for custody of their son — and she was feeling sorry for him?

I do need a vacation, she decided as they left the restaurant.

"See ya later, Juli," Mark said as he headed for Customer Service.

She nodded and, watching him go, she couldn't say who she pitied more at that moment, Mark J. or Stacie Rollins.

As usual, Julia didn't take a lunch break. She was too busy. Her paperwork was piling up and computers were going down. She was constantly interrupted and called away from one job to another. A program error here, an equipment problem there. Julia was only too glad for Angela, who followed her with spare keyboards, while Julia pushed a cart filled with extra monitors and hard drives.

"If Joan Miller spilled soda on her keyboard again, I'm writing her up!" Julia fumed.

"No, it's her monitor, this time," Angela replied.

Julia sighed. She'd never get to her paperwork today. After replacing the malfunctioning equipment, she had to check on a program error in Customer Service. Apparently, the "bugs" weren't all out of the new program yet. And here, Julia had thought she'd gotten everything up and running perfectly.

She wondered what Mark would have to say about her less-than-efficient program. Perhaps he would side with Stacie and insist the old program be reloaded. Except the new program had so many more capabilities . . .

It was nearly five o'clock when Julia got to Customer Service. "Sorry I'm late in getting here," she told Mark sincerely. "I've had some equipment problems."

"That's okay. The program error, whatever it is, doesn't seem to be getting in anyone's way for the time being."

She nodded. That's what one of Stacie's employees had said when they made the initial call for help, so she had put it last on today's priority list.

Sitting down at a vacant workstation, Julia proceeded to enter the computer system. Then, out of the corner of her eye, she spotted Stacie and turned to say hello. The sight that greeted her, however, stopped any words from forming. There, sitting across the aisle at another workstation, was Stacie Rollins, wearing one of the tightest, shortest skirts Julia had ever seen on a woman. Her low-cut, sheer blouse was equally remarkable.

It was then that Julia recalled Stacie saying she hoped to impress Mark with her looks since she wouldn't impress him with her computer skills.

"It's about time you got here, Julia!" Stacie declared, suddenly taking notice of her. In spite of her words, Stacie was smiling and seemed in a good mood.

"Not to worry," Julia said, recovering from her initial shock. "I'll fix the program error. I hope it didn't cause too many problems for your department."

"We worked around it." Stacie walked across the aisle and leaned over the side of the mahogany-veneered workstation. Julia forced herself not to grimace at the thought of Stacie's short skirt creeping any higher. "Mr. BC isn't such a bad guy," she whispered.

"Oh, well, that's good," Julia replied rather generically while she wished that Stacie wouldn't lean forward quite so far. Then she wondered how Mark had endured Stacie and her mini skirt all day. She was attractive in the outfit, even if it was grossly inappropriate for the office.

Obviously Mark handled things well enough, Julia decided, if Stacie isn't insulted. Maybe he even enjoyed working with Stacie today. Julia's sarcastic thoughts caught in her heart ✝ she had already sensed Mark's deep love for the Savior and his desire to obey God's Word. So how had Mark handled the likes of Stacie Rollins today?

Julia worked on the PC while Stacie walked off to gather her things.

"Well, it's almost five-thirty," she stated minutes later, slinging her delicate, leather purse over a slender shoulder. "Good night, Julia."

"See you tomorrow."

Julia looked for Mark as Stacie left the department. Two workstations away, he was sitting beside a male customer service representative, looking engrossed in whatever the other man was saying. Somehow Julia felt relieved that Mark's gaze hadn't followed Stacie.

Julia fought to bury her personal struggle and concentrate on the job before her. She managed to work diligently, and the next time Julia glanced at her watch it was nearly seven o'clock. She had corrected the program error —or at least she was reasonably sure she had. Time would tell. If the second-shift employees didn't have any problems, she would know she had been successful.

Mark came over as Julia stood, preparing to leave. "All done?"

She nodded, thinking that Mark looked tired. "Have you had a hard day?"

He shrugged.

"Stacie seemed to have fared all right. She told me you're not such a bad guy after all."

Mark grinned. "I do my best at not being a bad guy, that is."

Julia smiled and then momentarily contemplated as she chewed on her lower lip. "Can I ask you something, Mark? Something personal?"

"Sure. Fire away."

"Well . . . how did you handle it today? I mean . . . as a single man, a Christian man . . . and Stacie, dressed as she was . . . ?"

Mark's smile waned. "She really wasn't a distraction to me, Juli, if that's what you're getting at."

Julia was momentarily thoughtful. "Does that type of thing happen often? Business women trying to impress you with their looks instead of their diligence?"

132

Mark shrugged. "Now and then."

She nodded, coming to understand the reason behind the wedding ring he insisted upon wearing. "It must be very difficult for you sometimes," she murmured, lowering her chin. She ran a finger over the keyboard in front of her, as her heart went out to him for the second time that day.

"Yes, it is sometimes. But as a single, Christian woman, you must experience the same thing from time to time. Take Driscoll for instance."

Surprised, Julia looked up. "I'm not interested in Ken."

"I know you're not. And I have no interest in Stacie, other than to get her input on how this department functions as a whole."

Mark smiled so tenderly into her eyes then, that Julia felt as if her heart was out on a line and he was reeling it in. Slowly, ever so slowly.

"Will you have dinner with me, Juli?" he suddenly asked.

"I'd love to."

The evening was warm and smells of early summer were in the air — budding trees, blooming flowers, and smoke from backyard grills.

Julia walked beside Mark as they strolled back to Weakland Management. They both had left their cars in the parking structure and decided to walk the mile or so to the restaurant since the evening weather was so delightful.

"So, you're on vacation next week," Mark said, though it sounded more like a question.

Julia nodded. "I haven't been on a week-long vacation for years," she admitted. "I always make plans, but then something happens with the computer system and I end up either cutting my vacation time in half or not going at all. But I always manage to give Jesse a vacation. A few days here, a few days there. We sort of 'vacation' all summer long."

"Well, that's good. But aren't any of your employees capable of managing the computer system for a week?"

"Sure, they're capable. I just feel guilty for leaving them with the problems, I guess."

"For shame, Juli," Mark admonished her lightly. "Even you need a good chunk of time away from your work."

She grinned. "That's what Barb said, too. So, okay, I'm going on vacation, already!"

They shared a laugh and continued walking as an amiable silence fell over them. Julia resisted the urge to slip her hand into Mark's. How often had they walked together like this during their high school days? Except they would be holding hands . . . .

Julia shoved hers into the pockets of her suit jacket instead.

"Do you think you'll tell Jesse while you're on vacation?" Mark asked, breaking her silence.

"Yes, I'll tell him," she replied, noting the edge in her own voice. She tried to swallow it down. "He's going to have to learn about his father sooner or later, may as well be sooner." She paused. "Are you still holding that threat over my head?"

In the dusk of the evening, Julia saw him purse his lips thoughtfully. "No, I'm not going to hold that threat over your head. I'm sorry I ever made it." He paused. "I'm just anxious to meet my son. Is that unreasonable? It seems I've waited forever for the day to come. Even though I knew about Jesse a year ago, I wanted to wait until I talked to you before I entered his life. Like I said, I wanted you to tell me about him, Juli. I wanted to hear about our son from you."

Julia sighed. "Well, now you know."

"And you're not happy about it, are you?"

"I never said that."

"Juli, what are you afraid of, anyway?"

"Afraid .⌐?" She let the word hang between them in the evening summer air as she wondered how she could ever voice her innermost fears to him. Hadn't she shared her heart and soul with Mark before? And look what happened then. He betrayed her trust.

"Guess I hit a nerve, huh?" Mark finally said when she didn't reply.

"Sort of. Look, Mark, I forgave you. I even believe you, but I guess I'm just not ready to trust you yet. That's going to take a while."

The silence, no longer amicable, seemed to grow between them, lasting until they reached Weakland Management. Then finally Mark said, "I'm not a monster, Juli." His voice sounded weary or maybe heavy with emotion, she couldn't tell. And she couldn't see his face because of the encroaching darkness of the night.

When she didn't reply, Mark said roughly, "Come on. I'll walk you to your car."

☨ Chapter 10

Julia arrived at work shortly after eleven-thirty the next morning due to a downtown business seminar. She was still making some mental notes when Mark came up behind her.

"G'morning, Juli. It is still morning, isn't it?" Beside her now, he looked at his wristwatch. "Yep. It's still morning."

Julia gave him a curious look, noting that he didn't look very happy.

"Where have you been?" he wanted to know.

"At a seminar." She frowned now because he was frowning so hard.

"Did I know about this seminar?"

"I don't know. Were you supposed to? I mean, I was scheduled to attend it months ago. Bill knew about it."

"He didn't have it written down on his calendar and he was looking for you."

"Oh . . . well, I'm sorry about that. I'm sure I cleared it with him. In fact,

137

Weakland Management prepaid my way . . . Mark? What's wrong?"

"Was Driscoll at the seminar, too?"

"Ken?" Julia shook her head. "It was a seminar on technological advancement in computer programming. Why would Ken attend?"

"He's not here."

"Well, Ken wasn't with me."

They had reached IS now and Mark continued to walk with her all the way to her office. He waited while she unlocked the door and then he followed her inside.

"Do you have a syllabus or something from this seminar?"

Setting her attaché case on her desk, Julia whirled around to face him. "Do you think I'm lying? And what's it to you, Mark? You're not my supervisor."

Mark lifted his brows. "I'm curious. Why are you so defensive?"

Julia paused, considering him. "I guess I just don't appreciate you questioning me like this."

Mark closed her office door. "Juli, I didn't know where you were this morning. Bill asked me if I had seen you and, since I hadn't, I began to wonder. Besides, that program error is still popping up in Customer Service."

"Oh no ." Julia leaned against her desk.

"I think I might know how to fix it, but I didn't dare do anything without you here."

Julia sighed. "Well, thanks for that, anyway."

He nodded. "So, when can you get to that program error?"

"Why are you attacking me?"

"Why are you taking it personal? This is a business and there's a department with a programming error."

Julia swallowed her retort and took a deep, calming breath. "I'll get to it right away," she said, forcing a soft tone of voice. Then she crossed the room and opened the door.

"Juli?"

She turned.

"Aren't you going to put this stuff away?" Mark asked, nodding toward her purse and attaché case.

She shrugged. "I'll put it away later." On that, she left her office with Mark still standing there.

Two o'clock that afternoon, Julia was in Sir Walter's, pouring herself a strong cup of coffee. She normally didn't drink coffee this late in the day, but it looked like it was going to be a long night. The program she had created for the Customer Service Department had all but crashed, and Julia was disappointed and frustrated.

Having filled her ceramic mug with the freshly-ground, steaming brew, Julia walked slowly back toward Customer Service and the workstation she'd been at, laboring diligently. She sat down and began to work on the computer program when Mark pulled up a chair beside her.

"Listen, Juli," he fairly whispered, "this isn't small-town Lyon, Illinois. You've got to lock up your stuff + your desk drawers, credenza and your office door from now on. Okay?"

She looked at him, puzzled. "Why?"

"Don't ask questions. I can't answer them right now. Just take my advice, okay?"

"You're serious, aren't you?"

"Extremely."

She nodded, feeling a little worried now. What was going on that had Mark whispering and acting suspicious? "Can I question you after hours?" she asked on a hopeful note.

Mark shook his head. "Sorry. You'll just have to ⌿ trust me, Juli." The statement had a ring of sarcasm to it.

Then he looked at her computer terminal. "Want some help?" he asked, his voice its normal pitch again.

"With trusting you or with the computer program?" she asked tartly.

Mark's expression said he wasn't amused. Standing, he walked off to the other side of the department.

The night wore on. Finally, around ten o'clock, the computer program was up and running, but very slowly. The second-shift employees were frustrated because they couldn't get their work done. Adding to their stress was the fact that Mark, for whatever reason, had decided to hang around. After the business dinner last week, several of the more rebellious employees dubbed him the company "spy" since he had access to Bill's "listening ear." Julia suspected that those same employees were the ones working tonight, in Security, Customer Service, and Data Processing — the only departments that had a second shift. And they did not look happy.

"So what happens if the computer crashes at eleven-thirty some night?" Mark asked, following her back to Information Systems.

"I carry my pager at all times. Security notifies me if something goes wrong."

He nodded, pursing his mouth and

looking pensive. "Do you have backups?"

Julia nodded. "Downstairs. Behind Security. The Central Processing Units, or CPUs, are in a standard climate-controlled room. That's where much of our information is stored."

"And only authorized personnel are allowed in there?"

Julia turned to look at him. "No, we don't lock it up. Employees from the Data Processing Department have to get in there. I've trained them to start certain programs on certain nights so the jobs can run all night and not hang up the computers during the day."

"Then maybe the employees from DP ought to lock it up," Mark suggested. "As a matter of fact, that's next on my list of recommendations. Locks."

"But, Mark, security officers are sitting right there."

"Would they stop an unauthorized employee from entering the CPU room?"

Julia shrugged. She honestly didn't know. She'd never had a reason to question anyone here at Weakland Management. Who would want to go into the CPU room anyway? Half the time, she and her employees had to practically beg the people in DP to go in there and run the programs.

Entering her office, Julia gathered her things and prepared to go home. She was suddenly glad that Jesse was up north with her parents, although there had been other late nights when he stayed at Barb and Glen's house. In any case, she missed him. The apartment was much too quiet without him around.

As she left her office, Mark stepped aside so she could lock the door. Then he followed her through the department and waited while she locked the outer door.

"I'll walk you to your car."

"I can manage."

"I insist."

She gave him a curious glance, but his expression revealed very little. "Did you ever find Ken today?"

"Yes. Apparently he had a 'power brunch' with some clients and didn't bother to let Bill know about it. He's still upstairs . . . working, I guess. Frankly, I don't know what he's doing. Shuffling papers, maybe." He looked over at her as she struggled to understand where all the animosity was coming from. "That's why I'm escorting you to your car, Juli."

She lifted her brows. "Because of Ken?" Smiling, she shook her head. "He's harmless, Mark."

He laughed tersely. "So he's harmless, but I'm a monster?"

"Mark, I never said you were a monster."

"You didn't have to," he told her as they reached the parking lot. "Your actions speak louder than words."

Julia didn't reply. She was too tired to spar with Mark.

"Oh, come on, Juli, you need to be spiritually fed," Barb told her the next night. "Come to the worship service tonight. Glen and I will pick you up."

"But I just got home from work. It's six-thirty."

"You've got a whole half hour to get ready."

Julia sighed, but she knew trying to talk Barb out of dragging her to the midweek worship service was futile. Unless she had a legitimate business meeting, was sick or dying, Barb accepted no excuses.

"We can be at your place by seven."

"All right," Julia said in a note of resignation.

She shrugged out of her navy blue, linen suit jacket and walked into her bedroom. There she changed from her matching linen skirt and peach-colored silk blouse into a full denim dress and casual flats.

The midweek worship service wasn't formal. Next Julia brushed her hair out and wondered if Mark would be there tonight. He had enjoyed the Sunday service?

Mark. What was with that man anyway? Julia hadn't a clue. Since yesterday he had been curt with her to the point of being downright unfriendly. And Ken . . .

Julia sighed, touching up her makeup. Ken was going out of his way to flirt with her which only seemed to fuel Mark's already fiery temperament.

Men, she thought with a sigh. *Can't live with 'em, can't live without 'em . . .*

Barb and Glen were precisely on time, Glen at the wheel of his GMC Suburban.

"Hi, you guys," Julia said, climbing into the backseat.

"Hi, yourself," Glen said with a smile. "Barb has been thinking about joining the choir again, so she's been warming up."

"There's practice tonight," she said informatively.

Glen snorted. "Guess that means you and I will have to fellowship after service tonight, Juli."

"Okay." She smiled, squelching the urge for an early night at home and a hot bubble bath.

For the remainder of the drive to church,

Barb sang "It Is Well With My Soul" while Glen hummed along, and Julia was reminded of how much she loved these two people. They had provided a firm foundation for her at a time when she thought her whole world was falling apart. How could she ever repay them? She couldn't. It was as simple as that! Julia knew the Frenches wouldn't want any payment, at least not in the monetary sense. *Dear God, please show me a way that I can repay Barb and Glen for all they've done for Jesse and me over the years.*

They arrived at church and Glen let the ladies out before he drove back into the lot and parked the Suburban. Julia followed Barb into the church, then to a pew where they sat down. The service was about to begin.

Glen appeared and when Julia looked up and prepared to make room for him in the pew, she saw that Mark was with him. He gave her a tight smile before sitting beside Glen.

"I'm glad you came, son," Glen said.

"I almost didn't," Mark replied, causing Julia to wonder. She exchanged looks with Barb who smiled back at her lovingly.

The worship service began with singing praises to God, followed by a brief, life-application message from the Bible. Next, requests were taken from those who had special burdens or needs and then everyone broke into small groups for prayer. When it was over, Barb went to choir practice and Glen was called away by a fellow parishioner.

"Can I speak with you for a few minutes, Juli?" Mark asked, standing at the end of the pew.

"Sure."

They walked outside, where the evening sun was just beginning to set. They made their way through the parking lot, toward Glen's Suburban. The church had been built on the outskirts of Menomonee Falls where there were still a few farms and fields left.

"This kind of reminds me of Lyon," Mark murmured.

Julia nodded. She had been reminded of Lyon, too, after she first started attending this church with Barb and Glen.

When they reached the truck, Mark turned and faced her. "Juli, I'm sorry for the way I've been acting the last couple of days." He looked down at the pavement for several long moments before his gaze met hers again. "I know you've never called me a monster to my face, but that's the way you make me feel sometimes. My intentions are honorable. Really. I've tried to show you that, but you still seem suspicious."

Julia didn't know what to say. She supposed he was right: she was suspicious. But that was only because she had so much to lose.

"Look, Juli, I don't want to fight anymore." Mark took a step closer. "When you and Driscoll didn't show up for work yesterday morning, I imagined you two were together somewhere and it riled me."

Julia gave him an incredulous stare. "Mark, I told you . . . there is nothing between Ken and me."

"I know, I know. But I was . . ." He paused as if struggling with what he wanted to say. "I was jealous, okay?" he finally blurted. "I'll admit it . . . and quit laughing!"

"I'm not laughing," Julia said, biting her cheek. "Okay, I laughed a little. Sorry. But, Mark, it's so silly. I mean, Ken and I . . ." She shook her head. "He's not my type, all right?"

Mark smirked. "What kind of man is your type?"

She shrugged, feeling a mixture of embarrassment and discomfort. She had always thought that Mark was her type. Lately, however, she wasn't so sure. She didn't know him anymore.

"There's that silence again. Like a wall." Mark shook his head. "Juli, you build them better than Nehemiah."

"Will you give me some time?"

"Time to fortify your walls and keep me out for good? I do want a relationship with my son, you know. It would be nice if you and I could at least be friends."

"I agree. But I need time to get reacquainted with you."

Mark considered her for a few moments through a narrowed gaze. "All right, that's fair," he finally said, heaving a tired-sounding sigh. "Maybe I did come barreling into your life. I suppose I should apologize for that along with my over-zealousness about meeting Jesse." He smiled then, and it was so charming and sincere that Julia's heart raced. "Guess I need to be like Joshua, huh? If I'm patient and trust God, those walls will come tumbling down. I'd do that for you, Juli. No problem."

She was touched by Mark's sensitivity.

"As for our close proximity at Weakland Management . . . well, I'd resign, but Bill has a lot of money invested in me."

Julia tipped her head to one side. "So what do you propose?"

"I propose a strictly professional relationship at work and a . . . well, whatever develops after that on our personal time."

Julia lifted a brow. "That means no running me over in the hallway."

Mark laughed. "Oh, all right." His tone beheld a note of feigned reluctance.

Julia smiled. "Okay, your proposal sounds reasonable to me."

"Should we shake on it?" Mark held out his right hand.

Julia slipped her hand into his. "You've got a deal, Mr. Henley."

His grip tightened. "But you've got to promise me that you'll be very careful at work right now, Juli, all right? No more working late by yourself. Lock up your belongings and your office . . ."

"Mark, you're scaring me."

"I don't mean to. I just wanted to give you a warning. Be aware." Still holding her hand, he pulled her closer to him. "It's just commonsense stuff, really — and I can't explain it right now. But I will someday. Someday soon." His blue eyes darkened with seriousness then. "Promise me, Juli. Promise me you'll be careful."

Looking up into Mark's face, she momentarily contemplated his request. It wasn't outrageous, only confusing. But what harm could there be in promising Mark she'd be "careful" at work? She was always careful!

"Juli . . . ?"

She gave him a little smile. "All right, Mark. I promise."

Chapter 11

When her office door slammed shut, Julia looked up suddenly from her computer. "Stacie . . . ?"

"I wanted you to be the first to know," she said with a toss of her head and wide grin. She shoved a memo at Julia.

"What's this?"

"An announcement. Read it."

Julia did and when she finished, she looked back at Stacie and smiled. "Congratulations. You've been promoted to the Director of the Customer Service Department."

Stacie smiled back at her. "I told you middle management is on its way out. But we've got one smart business consultant, Juli. He's advising Bill to make us all directors!"

Julia laughed softly. "How's that suppose to save Weakland Management any money?"

"Beats me. But as long as it's not my job in jeopardy, I don't care."

Julia rolled her eyes. Typical response from Stacie.

"Well, TGIF and have a good weekend," she said, moving toward the door. "You're on vacation next week, aren't you?"

Julia nodded.

Stacie chuckled. "Better rest up. Your week with Mr. BC is coming."

"Thanks for reminding me," Julia said facetiously.

"You bet."

On that, Stacie left the office and Julia forced her thoughts back to her work. She had to get her department's payroll done and handed in by the end of the day, and she didn't want to stay much after five o'clock. Today was Friday, after all, and Barb and Glen would be waiting for her since they were driving up to Minoqua tonight.

Their last conversation weighed heavily on Julia's heart once again. "Ask him," Barb had urged. "Ask Mark to come up for a few days."

Julia stared blankly at the computer screen. She'd been debating the idea ever since Barb had suggested it, crazy as it was — or was it? Since Wednesday night, she and Mark had been getting along very well. They had eaten dinner with the

Frenches last night and then they went for a walk.

Julia pushed her thoughts away and finished the payroll. She printed out the information, locked her office door, and took the report up to Jerry Fein. Then she entered Mark's office.

He glanced at his watch. "Four fifty-seven, Juli. Barb will tan your hide if you're late tonight."

She grinned. "I've still got three minutes."

He chuckled.

"Mark, I, uhm, wondered if I could ask you something." Julia lowered her voice. "Something personal."

"Sure. What's on your mind?"

"Well, you know I'm on vacation next week . . ."

"Yes."

"And Barb thought that it might be nice if you came up for the Fourth of July. I'll talk to Jesse immediately, of course, but I don't expect a bad reaction. He's curious about you — his father."

Mark pursed his lips thoughtfully as he considered the offer. "What about you? This is your vacation, Juli, do you really want me to impose?"

"You're not imposing. I'm inviting."

"Because Barb put you up to it?"

Julia paused for a long, pensive moment. She thought about their walk last night and how they had laughed over fond memories. "No. I . . . I'd like you to come," she finally said. She could feel her cheeks warming pink, and she hoped she didn't look as stupid as she felt — like a sixteen-year-old girl asking the cutest boy in the class to the "Turn-A-Bout" dance, where the girls ask the guys.

"Well, thanks, Juli."

She shrugged, wanting to appear nonchalant. "I sort of figured you'd be working Friday."

"I can take Friday off."

Julia couldn't help but smile.

"Do you think Jesse is really going to be all right with the news about me?"

She nodded, feeling confident about at least that much. "Jesse is a well-adjusted kid, Mark, and you and I have been getting along —"

"And I think that's important for Jesse to see."

"Exactly." Julia rose from the chair. "How about if I call you on Wednesday night? We can confirm our plans then."

Mark shook his head. "Call me Wednesday afternoon — better yet, I'll call you."

Mark grabbed a pen, and Julia gave him the phone number. He seemed so excited that Julia had to smile, even though there was trepidation pumping through her veins with every beat of her heart. What if Jesse preferred Mark to her and decided he wanted to live with his dad? What if Mark decided he wanted complete custody? What if, because he was in child care so much with her working her way through school and her career, Mark found her mothering skills lacking?

"Change your mind?" Mark asked as if divining her thoughts.

Julia shook her head. She didn't know how to voice her silly insecurities. And, yes, they were silly. Yes, she was insecure . . . and, yes, she was frightened!

"I wish you'd talk to me, Juli," Mark said wistfully as he walked around his desk and stood beside her. "I feel like a wall is going up before my very eyes."

Julia managed a smile and shook her head. "No, Mark, I'm entertaining ridiculous thoughts which I shouldn't even be thinking."

He frowned. "Hmm." Then a smile broke through, reminding Julia of a sunbeam on a cloudy day. "Well, stop it," he teased. "Let's have fun next weekend!"

"Okay," Julia smiled broadly in spite of herself.

Mark was smiling, too, as he walked her to the door. "Take care."

She nodded and left his office.

Then she caught a glimpse of Ken from the corner of her eye. She turned and saw that he was watching her intently so she waved. "See you in a week. I'm going on vacation. I mean, I'm really going this time. And not just for a day or two, but a real vacation!"

"I'm very disappointed in you, Julia," he replied, lofting a brow.

She chuckled inwardly at the sarcasm, knowing it came from a workaholic who would probably never think of taking time off from his career. Julia knew the feeling well.

"Have a good weekend anyway, Ken," she quipped before walking away.

She never saw the exchange that went on behind her back between Mark and Ken — the look of warning, the glare of open resentment.

"Mom, the lake is freezing up here!" Jesse declared the next morning at breakfast.

Julia smiled at her son. "We've had a

cold and rainy spring, Jess. I guess that explains it."

"Fishing's good, though," Roy replied, taking a bite of his homemade cinnamon roll. "We've had fish twice this week for supper. Isn't that right, Jesse?"

The boy nodded. "They were big ones, too, Mom. Really big."

Julia furrowed her brows. "Sounds like a fish story to me."

Her parents chuckled while Jesse insisted that the fish were "really big."

"And how are things at work, Juli?" Caroline asked, taking a sip of her coffee.

"Much better, Mom."

Roy looked across the table at her from beneath his bushy gray brows. "I hate to even ask what that means."

Julia sobered. "It means it's time to forgive and forget, Dad."

Roy narrowed his gaze. "Never!"

"What are we talking about?" Jesse wanted to know. "And how come you're so mad all of a sudden, Grandpa?"

"Never mind, son," Roy replied. He glanced back at Julia. "I've worked very hard to protect you all these years. I don't want to see you get hurt again — or any of us get hurt again." He nodded sideways at

Jesse. "I especially don't want to see him getting hurt."

"Me? Why would I get hurt?" Jesse asked, obviously trying to understand the adult conversation. "Are you talking about the time I went down to the lake by myself, Grandpa? But I know how to swim."

"No, no, son . . ."

"Jesse, will you go out to Uncle Glen's truck and bring in the rest of my things?" Julia asked sweetly. "I'm sure I left something in there last night. It was dark and I couldn't see to grab everything."

Reluctantly, the boy nodded, though he looked a little confused. "Can I say hi to Uncle Glen and Aunt Barb, too?"

"Sure."

Julia watched him go, waiting for him to get down the hill before she turned back to her father. "Mark wants to be part of Jesse's life, Dad, and I think that's only fair. He's Jesse's father. He has that right."

Roy's face reddened with anger. "Don't talk about rights where Mark is concerned. He forfeited his rights twelve years ago."

"That's how I felt too initially, but Mark is a different man these days." Juli smiled, shaking her head at the irony. She was defending Mark, of all people!

She stood and walked over to the

coffeemaker which was on the counter next to the sink. She filled her mug. "Dad, I think you should know that I've invited Mark to spend the Fourth of July with us . . . up here."

"You . . . what!" Now Roy was standing. He shook his head adamantly. "No. Absolutely not!"

"He'll stay with Barb and Glen," she continued despite his reply. "They were actually the ones who thought it would be a good idea. And I agreed. Mark and Jesse can get acquainted."

"Bad idea, Juli." Roy still shook his head. His gray hair was thinning on top, even though he combed it back in an effort to conceal the fact. He was a large man, with broad shoulders and muscular arms from years of heavy lifting and hard work. But beneath the gruff, Julia knew there was a man of sensitive heart and spirit, though he didn't share her Christian faith — yet. Julia knew that she could probably talk her father into buying swamp land in Florida if she truly had her mind set on it.

She sipped her coffee, considering him as he stared out the screen of the back door. "Mom said she told you about the letters."

"Yeah, she told me. You two are ganging

up on me . . . as usual."

"We are not ganging up on you, Roy," Caroline said, still enjoying her breakfast despite the commotion around her.

"Look, Dad," Julia said carefully, "you may as well get used to the idea. Mark is in our lives to stay . . . at least I hope so."

Roy swung around and glared at her. "You hope so?"

"For Jesse's sake," Julia clarified.

"Oh, and I suppose the next thing you'll tell me is that you're still in love with him."

Julia lowered her gaze to the coffee mug between her hands, hoping to hide her sudden discomfort. Part of her wanted to debate the comment, yet she honestly couldn't do it.

"I don't believe it!" Roy murmured.

"Dad, please, will you give Mark just one more chance? For Jesse's sake."

"And who's going to tell Jesse?"

"I will."

Caroline had finished her breakfast and was now clearing the table. "I think Jesse is going to be excited about meeting Mark." She looked up then, and her mind seemed far away. "You know, I can remember when Mark was Jesse's age." She smiled fondly. "He was such a sweet boy."

"What do you mean, 'sweet boy'?" Roy

asked, frowning heavily. "He and his older brother were always getting into trouble."

"Oh, they were not!" Caroline declared. "They were just being boys. Ours were just as mischievous, Roy."

"No, they weren't," he muttered irritably.

Julia had to chuckle. "Yes, they were, Dad." A moment of silence passed. "Did Mom tell you that Mark and his family are Christians now and that his parents are back together?"

"Yes." Roy shook his head once more. "Who would have ever called that one, huh?" He paused, then, and considered Julia thoughtfully. "So you're really going to allow Mark visiting privileges?"

Julia nodded.

"And he's really coming up here for the Fourth of July weekend?"

"That's right, Dad, although I wish that you'd concede to it."

"Oh, I'll concede to it," Roy said with a glint of warning in his eyes. "But I'm going to threaten that boy within an inch of his life. If he ever does anything to hurt my family again, he'll have to deal with me! Won't matter if he runs off to the other side of the world this time, either. I'll find him!"

Julia smiled.

★ ★ ★

The next afternoon was warm and the sunshine glistened off the lake, making the water look like fine crystal. From where Julia sat on the pier next to Jesse, she could feel the warm rays penetrating her skin like a deep-heating massage. It felt comforting.

She turned to Jesse now, wondering what he was thinking. She had just begun to tell him about his father.

"So you and . . . my dad went to school together?"

"That's right. And your dad was on the football team. He was the best, too, and that's when I fell in love with him."

"Then what happened?"

"Well, your dad finished school a year before I did and he went to work for Grandpa at his gas station and garage. The next year, after I finished school, your dad and I planned to get married." Julia paused, thinking that telling Jesse about Mark wasn't nearly as painful as she had thought it would be. "Well, the time came for us to get married, but then your dad changed his mind. He decided he needed to go to college before he got married. So he went away and we never got married, and that's when I learned that I was going to have a baby."

"Me?"

Julia nodded. "You see, Jesse, your dad and I . . . well, we sinned because we . . . Well, we were acting like a husband and wife, except we weren't married, and that's sin. We made a mistake, but, Jesse," she said emphatically, "you were never a mistake. Do you understand that? You have always been a very special blessing to me . . . and all of our family, too." Julia smiled. Then, putting an arm around his shoulders, she leaned over and kissed his cheek. "I loved you from the minute you were born!"

The boy shrugged, looking embarrassed. "Aw, Mom . . ."

Straightening, Julia concluded her story. "I never told your dad about you because I thought he didn't care. But he does. And now he wants to meet you. What do you think?"

"I don't know." Jesse seemed thoughtful as he gazed down into the water. "Is my dad nice?"

"Yes."

"Is he rich?"

Julia thought about it. "I guess I'm not sure if he's 'rich,' but he's probably doing all right financially."

"Do you like him?"

"Yes," Julia replied carefully.

"Do you love him?"

Julia rolled her eyes. How come she had a feeling Jesse would ask her that? But she was prepared.

"Jesse," she began, "my feelings for your dad don't matter when it comes to your relationship with him. Your dad wants to be part of your life, and I think you should at least meet him and give him a chance."

Jesse seemed to think it over before he started on his next series of questions. "What's his name?"

"Mark Thomas Henley."

"Hey, Mark is my middle name!"

"You were named for your dad."

"What's he look like?"

"Well, he's about as tall as Grandpa, and he still sort of looks like a football player . . ."

"Grandpa looks like a lineman."

Julia bit her lip in effort not to chuckle. Her father did have a bit of a tummy on him now, due to his retirement and her mother's good cooking. "Your dad isn't that big, Jess," she finally replied. "And you kind of look like him."

"Does he like jokes?"

"Loves them."

"Does he have a dog?"

"I don't know, but you could ask him."

Jesse's questions didn't stop for the next three days, and he took turns following the adults around, asking them about his dad. Julia was only too grateful for her mother who provided Jesse with story after story about Mark's growing up years. And, when he finally called Wednesday afternoon, Jesse behaved as though he knew his dad very well.

"Mom says you've got a real neat old car," Jesse told Mark, holding the receiver to his ear as Julia sat by, watching, listening and praying that all would go well. "Uncle Glen says he's got some fireworks that we can set off on the Fourth of July." Jesse paused and then his eyes grew round. "Mom!" he whispered, holding his hand over the phone, "Dad says he's got some fireworks, too!"

"That'll be fun," Julia replied with an encouraging nod.

"Okay, here's Mom." Jesse handed her the telephone unceremoniously before running off to inform his grandparents about the fireworks.

"Hi, Mark," Julia said, putting the receiver to her ear.

"Did I hear correctly? He's calling me

'Dad' already?" There was a note of amazement in Mark's voice.

"Yes, well, he's got the scoop on you now." Julia chuckled and explained about Jesse's inquiring mind and how Grandma McGowan was stimulating it with stories of days gone by. Minutes later, Mark was chuckling too.

"Well, I can't wait to meet him, Juli. He sounds like a neat kid."

"He is."

"My parents will be thrilled. They can't wait to meet Jesse, either. I haven't really thought that far ahead, but I'd like to take him to Springfield sometime."

Tiny prickles of apprehension climbed Julia's spine at Mark's words "take him," and yet it only seemed logical that Mark would want his parents to meet Jesse. She had decided to share him, and now she would just have to follow through on her decision.

Mark asked for directions to Minoqua then, and Julia gave them. "I'll see you later this week," he promised. "I'm leaving here right at five o'clock, so I'll get up there around ten-thirty or eleven. I hope that's not too late."

"No, it's not too late," Julia replied, swallowing the urge to ask how things were going at Weakland Management. This week Mark was sitting in with Jon Maxwell and the data processing department. But she was on vacation. She wasn't supposed to think about work. "See you later, Mark."

Julia hung up the telephone, and when she turned, her father was standing there in the kitchen, eyeing her speculatively.

"You're setting yourself up for a fall, Juli," he said. "I can see it coming and, just like the last time, I'll have to pick up the pieces."

"No, Dad, don't say that." Without even knowing it, Roy McGowan had voiced her darkest fear.

As she watched her father walk away, Julia noticed the slight bend to his shoulders. It seemed like a sad bend, too, like one that had carried an enormous burden for a long, long time.

Oh, dear God, I just want to do the right thing by Mark and Jesse. Please don't let this be the second biggest mistake of my life.

Chapter 12

It was nearly eleven o'clock when Julia heard Mark's car pull onto the gravel road. Sitting in the kitchen, she and Jesse had been waiting up for Mark, playing "Crazy-8s" to pass the time. But when his car's headlights briefly flashed through the kitchen windows, Jesse looked across the table at her, wearing an anxious expression.

"Mom . . . ?"

"Don't worry, Jess," she said with a smile. "You'll like your dad. You'll see." Julia felt somewhat apprehensive, but she wasn't about to let her son know it. "Come on. Let's go meet him."

They walked outside, Julia's arm around Jesse's shoulders. After days of excitement, the boy seemed suddenly shy and reluctant as Mark climbed out of his car.

"Welcome," Julia said neighborly. "I'm glad you found the cabins all right."

"You gave great directions." Mark looked at the boy now standing in front of him. "You must be Jesse."

He nodded and an awkward silence ensued.

Julia decided to break the ice a bit. "This is your father, Jesse, Mark Henley." She looked back at Mark, his features barely visible under the yard light.

He held out his hand. "I'm glad to finally meet you, Jesse."

The boy considered, first the outstretched hand, and then the man. Finally he clasped Mark's hand. "I'm glad to finally meet you, too." His voice sounded stiff and formal.

Julia turned to Mark. "You'll be staying with Barb and Glen. Jesse and I can help you with your things, and then we'll walk you down to their cabin."

"Sounds good. Here, Jesse, will you carry the bag of fireworks for me?"

Julia smiled. Mark couldn't have picked a better task. Jesse perked right up.

"Wow! You brought all these?"

"Uh-huh."

"Can I help you set some off?"

"I think you probably can . . . if your mother says it's all right."

"Is it, Mom?"

"Well . . . is it really safe, Mark?"

"Sure. I'll be right there with him."

"C'mon, Mom, plee-ease."

Julia laughed softly, deciding that she could now sympathize with her father and how he must have felt all those years being constantly coerced by the two women he loved most. "Well, we'll see," she finally replied.

Jesse turned to Mark with an air of confidence. "Whenever my mom says 'we'll see' that means yes."

Mark chuckled. "Is that right?" He looked at Julia who was shaking her head at the both of them.

"Jesse, let's get your dad to Aunt Barb and Uncle Glen's cabin. I'm sure he's tired."

"Okay."

Jesse led the way with Mark trailing behind Julia. He wouldn't let her carry anything so she walked empty-handed down the narrow dirt trail that led to the cabin.

"Barb and Glen are sleeping," she whispered to Mark as they entered the dimly lit kitchen/dining room area. "You're in the back bedroom and the bathroom is right across the way."

Mark set down his suitcase. "I'm kind of keyed up from all the driving. Would it be okay if we just sat outside for a while?"

"Sure. Would you like something to eat first?"

Mark shook his head. "I stopped at a fast-food place on the way up."

"All right . . . well, let's all go sit on the pier for a while. It's so peaceful out there."

"Yeah, and I'll get my fishing pole!" Jesse declared. Then he stopped short. "Hey, do fish sleep?"

Julia furrowed her brows. "I don't know." She turned to Mark. "Do they?"

He smiled, looking amused. "Naw, fish don't sleep."

"Good!" Jesse was gone in an instant, promising to bring a flashlight along with his tackle box.

Julia sighed as she and Mark stepped out of the cabin. "He'll be up all night at this rate."

Mark chuckled. "Well, maybe he'll catch something and it'll be worth it."

The narrow dirt path continued from the Frenches' cabin on down to the lake. The moon was only a half-sliver in the sky, but a relatively sufficient guiding light.

"There's a long bench on the end of the pier," Julia said, pointing straight ahead. She noticed that Mark hadn't even changed after work — he wore a light-blue dress shirt, navy pants, and fine leather shoes.

"How's everything going at Weakland

Management?" she couldn't help but ask. "Any new developments?"

Mark looked at his watch. "Fifteen minutes."

Julia paused, standing in the middle of the pier. "What?"

"Fifteen minutes. I was wondering how long it would be before you brought up the subject of work. You waited a whole fifteen minutes. Good for you."

Julia tossed her head in indignation, putting her hands on her hips. "How would you like to take a swim, Mark Henley?"

Beneath the moonglow, she saw him grin. "If I go swimming, Juli-bean, you're coming with me."

She considered the challenge, smiling all the while. Oh! but she would like nothing better than to push Mark into the freezing cold lake with his dress clothes on! Of course, if he pulled her in with him, that wouldn't be so fun.

She sighed a dramatic breath of resignation. "All right, you win . . . for now."

Mark chuckled. "Know what? I can tell we're going to have a great time this weekend."

Julia was still shaking her head at him when Jesse returned, fishing pole in one

173

hand, his tackle box in the other. "Hey, wanna see all my lures?" he asked Mark enthusiastically.

"Sure."

Mark held the flashlight, while Jesse pulled out each lure, one by one, explaining where and when he got it and how many fish he had caught with it.

Julia looked on, marveling at the scene before her. Mark was here . . . with her . . . and Jesse! The makings of a family right before her eyes. But what would become of it?

Julia pushed her thoughts away and glanced out over the still, dark lake. She was afraid to pay the price for dreaming. She couldn't afford it.

"Hey, Juli, you falling asleep on us over there?"

She smiled from where she sat on the bench at the end of the pier. "No, I was just thinking."

"No thinking allowed. You're on vacation, remember?"

Julia laughed softly as Mark walked over and sat down beside her. Jesse was sitting a few feet away, his legs dangling off the pier while he fished.

"This is almost perfect, isn't it, Juli?" Mark murmured, his arm stretched out behind her, resting on the top of the bench.

He turned to her and, though Julia couldn't make out his features clearly, she sensed the intent expression on his face. He's going to kiss me, she thought, her heart pounding in anticipation and, yes, even longing.

"Hey, are you sure that fish don't sleep?" Jesse called over his shoulder, breaking the intensity of the moment.

Julia didn't know whether to feel disappointed or relieved.

Mark was chuckling under his breath. "I've never known fish to sleep, Jesse," he teased the boy, "but, in any case, I'm sure you just woke them up."

"Good!"

Mark chuckled again and even Julia had to laugh. It was obvious, Mark and Jesse were going to get along just fine.

They stayed on the pier for a good hour, until the wind felt cold and Julia's eyelids refused to stay open. She and Jesse said good-night to Mark at the Frenches' cabin and then climbed the hill to their own. Inside, Julia helped Jesse put away his fishing gear and then insisted that he wash up before going to bed.

"I like him, Mom," Jesse said, twirling the bar of soap between his hands.

"That's good," Julia said as a yawn escaped her. "Hurry up, Jess. I'm tired."

The boy finished in the bathroom and then Julia planted a good-night kiss on his cheek. She watched him walk into the bedroom next to her parents' and knew that he'd be up bright and early in the morning. He would most likely want to see his dad first thing.

A wry grin curved her mouth, and she hoped Mark was prepared to be awakened in about five hours.

The Fourth of July dawned bright and beautiful. The sun shimmered off the lake and the treetops waved in the warm breeze. Just as Julia had predicted, Jesse awoke and ran down to the Frenches' cabin to see his father. Barb came in about eight o'clock, chuckling all about it.

"And Mark seems impressed with Jesse, too," she said, looking pleased. "What a blessing."

Julia just nodded as she stood at the sink, drying the breakfast dishes while her mother washed them. Her father had been stomping around the kitchen all morning and she feared a positive reply would be like waving a red flag in front of an angry bull. Finally Roy announced that he and

Mark were going to have "a talk" and, with that, he left the cabin.

Julia glanced at her mother, feeling a good measure of alarm. "Should you stop him?"

"I should say not!" Caroline exclaimed and Barb agreed.

"Glen can keep Jesse occupied. It's high time Mark and your father had a talk."

Caroline seemed momentarily pensive. "You know, Juli, after Mark left, there were those times when you were up in your bedroom crying your heart out, and all of us, your brothers included, felt just wretched for you. But your father . . . well, I think he felt it even more deeply than the boys and me. I believe, in fact, that he was just as hurt as you were when Mark left. He thought of Mark as one of his own boys. So much so that he was willing to leave his service station to him — and that business meant a lot to your father."

Caroline washed a plate, still looking thoughtful. "But what I remember most," she continued, "is that your father would stand at your closed door, Juli, with tears falling down his cheeks. He was crying right along with you, but he didn't know how to comfort you because he was so hurt himself."

Julia had never heard this before and she was touched to tears. No wonder her father's anger at Mark had matched her own. No wonder he was so unwilling to let Mark back into their lives. He had been affected the same way she had. The only difference was, Julia knew the love of the Savior now, her father did not. Forgiving Mark hadn't come easily for her, but it had been possible because of Christ.

Barb sniffed, looking teary-eyed herself. "Oh, I just pray that Mark and Roy can work things out."

Julia nodded, still struggling to put her own emotions to rest.

Many long minutes passed, and she resumed drying the dishes and putting them away. Then she tuned in to Barb's merry chatter about the picnic this afternoon. And then, of course, the fireworks tonight.

"Oh, this will be so much fun," Barb crooned. Together the two older ladies sat down at the kitchen table to prepare the menu.

Listening to her mother and Barb, Julia had to smile. They were planning a veritable feast.

Then suddenly she spotted Mark and her father walking casually toward Mark's car. "Mom . . . ?" Julia wondered if her father were insisting that Mark leave, except he didn't have his suitcase and . . . and they were both smiling!

"What is it, dear?" Caroline came to stand beside her.

"Look."

"Oh . . ."

Barb was at Julia's other side now. She chuckled at the sight of Mark and Roy lifting the Impala's hood. "Looks like a budding friendship to me."

"Yes, and now the real discussion begins," Caroline added with a satisfied smile. "I've heard it before and it's amazing what men can talk about beneath the hood of a car."

Amusement danced in Barb's blue eyes. "Solve the world's problems, do they?"

"And then some!"

The women all laughed. Julia was downright amazed — if Mark could win her father, he must be sincere. Perhaps even trustworthy. After all, Roy McGowan was no fool — not even for a refurbished '66 Chevy Impala!

We'll see, she told herself. We'll just see . . .

By the time Mark and Roy came in from outside it was after noon, and Jesse and

Glen were sitting at the kitchen table, eating sandwiches. The party didn't start till three o'clock, so the "boys" insisted upon a "snack."

"Are there more of those?" Roy asked, nodding at Jesse's plate. Then he tossed Mark a clean rag with which he could wipe off his hands. "I'm starving."

"Coming right up," Caroline replied. "You too, Mark?"

"Yes, thanks."

Julia couldn't resist sending Mark a questioning look. She was eager to learn what happened between him and her father. But when Mark smiled at her, sending back an affectionate wink, Julia decided things must have gone well.

The rest of the afternoon was as pleasurable as the weather. Warm friends and sunny conversations. Glen took Mark, Jesse, and two of the neighbor boys for a ride in his motorboat. They cruised around the lake and, once they returned, all "the guys" sat on the pier and fished until it was time to fire up the grill.

After a supper of grilled hamburgers and bratwurst, baked beans, Jell-O, and chocolate brownies, the adults settled into lawn chairs near the lake and visited while the kids lit sparklers on the beach. One of the neighbor girls was in high school so she was awarded the job of holding the matches; however, adult supervision wasn't ever far away. Then, later, Mark and Jesse would set off the fireworks.

Julia noticed that Mark fit right in. The guests liked him and Jesse had already come to adore him. Mark was suddenly his hero and, likewise, Mark seemed captivated by his son.

Watching this, Julia had to admit she felt a stab of jealousy. But then she imagined how complicated it could have been if Mark and Jesse hadn't taken a liking to each other. She would have felt badly for the both of them, so she allowed herself the joy of witnessing father and son together, having a good time.

"Want a roasted marshmallow, Juli?" Mark asked, sitting in the lawn chair next to her. "Jesse's cooking."

She smiled. "Sure."

Mark nodded and cupped his hands around his mouth. "Make one for your mom, Jess," he called.

"Okay, *Dad*."

The way Jesse said "dad" was so cute it made Julia grin. It was a new word in his vocabulary, and he used it whenever he got the chance.

"Having fun?" Mark asked, turning to Julia.

"Yes, I'm enjoying myself today."

"Me, too. Especially since your dad and I talked things out. He hasn't said he forgives me — I think he's going to make me prove myself." Mark shrugged. "But I accept the challenge. Making amends with you and your family is that important to me."

Julia appreciated the remark. "I'm glad."

Mark sighed, looking around. "It's pretty up here."

She nodded.

"Do you get to come here often?"

"Oh, maybe a few times each summer."

"I think I'd be up here every weekend."

Julia shrugged. "I'm often on-call during the weekends."

"Which is going to change," Mark said emphatically.

She looked at him, raising questioning brows.

Mark sat back in his chair and crossed his legs. He wore faded blue jeans and a red-and-white striped T-shirt — very appropriate for the holiday. On his feet, he wore the latest, fashionable brand of athletic shoes, causing Jesse to want a pair just like "Dad's."

"Listen, Juli," he began, "you've got three employees, two of which can take turns carrying that pager."

"But —"

"And Jon Maxwell's department is going to help. In fact, Bill decided that Jon is going to —"

"He's going to . . . what?" Julia asked with a frown.

Mark paused. "Forget it, Juli. Let's not talk about work any more."

Julia opened her mouth to protest, but then Jesse presented her with a charred marshmallow.

"Here you go, Mom."

"Thanks," she said, looking at the burned thing. "You know, Jesse, I prefer my roasted marshmallows a golden brown. Could you cook another one for me?"

Jesse shrugged. "Okay."

Being a good sport, Mark volunteered to eat the burned one.

"Now, what about Jon's department?" Julia wanted to know after Jesse walked back toward the brick barbeque pit.

"Juli, let's not discuss it now. There will be plenty of time next week for us to discuss all the changes, all right?"

"All the changes . . . ?" Julia's voice trailed off as she considered what those words meant. "I missed a lot this past week, huh?" Insecurity suddenly gripped her heart.

"You didn't miss anything you can't catch up on next week."

Julia folded her arms across her chest and turned pensive. Jon Maxwell had his Masters Degree; she only had her Bachelors.

"Quit worrying, Juli," Mark whispered. "I'm sorry I even brought up the subject of work. You were actually beginning to relax."

She sighed and had to admit Mark was right. She had been slowly unwinding from all the day-to-day stress, but now it seemed pressing again.

"Lighten up, Juli," Mark teased her, "or I'll throw you in the lake."

She bit the inside of her cheek in an effort to keep from smiling. How could Mark do that to her? From worry to amusement in a single bound.

She looked over at him, meeting Mark's gaze. "You know? I'm glad you came up here," she said softly.

He smiled back in a way that made Julia's heart hammer. "So am I," he replied. "So am I."

Chapter 13

The next day, Friday, was as pleasant as its predecessor. Mark learned that there was a public stable off the main highway and wanted to take Jesse horseback riding. Jesse, of course, was all for the idea, especially since it was Mark who suggested it.

Then Mark insisted that Julia come along. He seemed to be working very hard at including her, and she appreciated his efforts. After all, he could demand that, since she'd had their son to herself for eleven years, he was entitled to at least a few hours. But he didn't. In fact, Mark was a perfect gentleman the entire afternoon.

Later that evening, after supper, Jesse fell asleep early. Julia's parents and the Frenches were playing their own simplified version of bridge at the kitchen table, which left Julia and Mark to themselves.

"Would you like to go for a walk?" she asked. "I'm feeling kind of restless."

"I'm feeling exhausted," Mark replied,

looking sheepish, "but I'll go for a walk anyway."

Julia smiled as they left the cabin and slowly walked down the gravel road. The air was mild and the sun was just beginning its descent in the western sky. There was still a good hour of daylight left.

"Are you really too tired, Mark?" Julia hoped he didn't feel obligated.

He shook his head. "No, I'm fine. In fact, I think the walk will do me some good. Stretch out my leg muscles. I have a feeling I'm going to be a little sore tomorrow."

"Sorry to hear that, cowboy," she quipped with a teasing smile.

Mark's expression was one of chagrin and Julia had to laugh. "You sure are sassy."

"Yes, so you've told me before."

They turned off the gravel road and onto the pavement of another, seldom-used road. On either side, a dense grove of trees grew so tall they seemed to touch the clouds. Julia inhaled deeply. The air felt so clean and fresh.

"You like it up here, don't you?"

She nodded. "I wish I'd make myself come up here more often."

Mark seemed to consider her comment

for several long moments as he gazed around them, wearing an appreciative expression. Julia could tell he liked it up here, too.

"I'm having a nice holiday," Mark said at last. "And you're a lot of fun to be around."

"Thanks. So are you."

Mark smiled. "I'm glad you feel that way. I guess I'd like to think we're friends." He paused. "Hey, Juli? Can I ask you something personal?"

She shrugged. "Sure."

Mark paused once more, seemingly to collect his thoughts. Finally, he asked, "Are you romantically involved with anyone? I mean, I asked about Driscoll, but . . . well, is there someone else? Someone in your Bible study perhaps?"

Julia figured he was asking because of Jesse. "No, I'm not involved with anyone."

"How come?"

"What?"

"How come? I mean, you're a lovely person, Juli. I'm actually surprised more men at Weakland Management aren't pestering you."

She smiled, feeling a bit embarrassed by his comment. "Oh, they used to, especially right after I started working there. But I wasn't interested in dating." She bent to pick a wild flower at the side of the road. "Relationships take so much time and effort," she said frankly, "and I just wasn't willing to make that kind of investment."

"Hmmm . . . so, let me get this straight. You haven't had a date in twelve years?"

Julia thought it over and then nodded. "Pretty pitiful, isn't it?"

Mark furrowed his brow, and Julia couldn't help but suddenly wonder if he were inquiring over her morals in order to gauge what kind of mother she'd been. Would Mark find her lacking? Did he think she was lying about not dating?

They walked for a few moments in silence and then Mark changed the subject completely.

"So how did you get interested in computers?"

"Well, after Jesse was born, I got a job as a clerk in a small computer store. I got interested in programming, so I decided to go to college. I figured programming would allow me to use some of my creativity. And it does."

Mark nodded. "Ever wish you weren't a . . . a career woman?"

Julia expelled a curt laugh. "Mark, I stopped wishing a long time ago."

His expression changed, and she sensed she'd somehow hurt his feelings. She hadn't meant to; she was just being honest.

She gave him a sweet smile, trying to console him. He smiled back then, and the tension between them vanished. They continued to walk down the road which circled around the property and ended up back on the gravel driveway. But when they reached the cabins, neither Julia nor Mark seemed to want to say good night, so they strolled down to the lake and onto the pier where they sat on the long wooden bench.

Mark stretched his arm out along the back of the bench behind her, and Julia felt warm and secure sitting so close beside him. She thought that something deep within her was awakening after being dormant for so very long. And that something, she decided, was a little frightening.

She folded her arms tightly in front of her, suddenly feeling terribly unsure of herself.

"Cold?" Mark had obviously noticed the cool breeze coming off the lake.

But Julia shook her head. "No, I'm okay."

Silence settled between them as they listened to the loons. And all the while, Julia was very aware of Mark's presence. She realized, then, that she had virtually turned off her feelings twelve years ago in effort to protect herself from ever getting hurt again. She had lied to herself, telling her heart she didn't care about Mark anymore. But, the truth was, she had loved Mark all along.

"You're awfully quiet," he remarked. "You didn't fall asleep on me, did you?" His arm fell onto her shoulder and he gave her playful shake.

Julia smiled. "I'm awake, I'm awake!"

She turned to consider him, his face just inches away, and her smile faded as an intense wave of emotion gripped her heart. Likewise, his blue eyes darkened with ardor.

"I never stopped loving you, Mark. I never stopped . . ." Tears pooled in Julia's eyes at the admission.

"Why are you crying?" Mark asked, wearing a confused frown. "What you just said is a wonderful thing. Juli?"

She was shaking her head. "But I don't want to love you."

Mark's frown deepened and there was an obvious look of hurt in his eyes, so Julia rushed on to explain.

"I'm afraid, Mark."

"Of what? Of me?" His tone sounded suddenly impatient.

"Yes! Mark, I don't want to get hurt again."

His features softened. "I won't hurt you, Juli. I've told you that already."

She swallowed the last of her emotion and wiped away an errant tear. "I'm having a hard time trusting you. I mean, I trusted you once before, and —"

"Juli, that was twelve years ago." Mark shook his head, looking exasperated. "I was nineteen and very confused . . . Juli, we've been through all this. I've apologized and you said you forgave me. What else is left?"

She chanced a look at him, then momentarily fretted, chewing on her lower lip. "What about Jesse?"

"What about him?"

She lifted her chin, remembering Mark's earlier questions about her dating experiences. "Are you going to fight me for custody?"

Mark's eyes widened as if he couldn't believe what he'd just heard. "Fight you?"

"I mean, if that's your plan I would like to know so I can prepare —"

"Julia!" He shook his head incredulously before his eyes bore into hers. "Juli, look at us. I'm sitting here with my arm around you, the moon is coming up over the lake, you just said you're still in love with me . . . we should be enjoying this moment. But instead you've poisoned it with your ridiculous suspicions!"

"I was trying to be honest with you, Mark. I was sharing my heart —"

He stood, the magic of the moment gone. "No, you weren't. You were slinging the past in my face — again."

"Not intentionally." She stood now, too. "I was merely trying to tell you my fears — so I can put them to rest." Anger suddenly overtook her emotions. "But you don't care about that, do you? All you care about is what you want, which is . . . oh!" she cried, throwing her hands in the air. "I don't even know what you want — and that's the problem!"

Even in the dimness of the evening, Julia could see Mark's eyes narrowing to dangerous slits. With hands-on-hips, she glared right back at him.

"How'd you like to go for a swim, Julia Rose McGowan?"

Her eyes widened at the question — the same she'd asked him two nights ago.

She tipped her head saucily. "If I go swimming, Mark," she mimicked, "you're going with me."

He stepped forward, obviously un-daunted.

"Mark, I'm serious." She pointed a warning at him. "Stay where you are."

Another step.

"I was nice to you and backed down," she said, feeling testy now since Mark seemed bent on throwing her into the lake. "I didn't push you in even though I would have loved to — Allen Edmonds and all."

One step closer.

Julia looked behind her heels then and realized that she was at the very edge of the pier. Maybe she'd jump and rob him of the satisfaction of pushing her in.

But the idea came too late. Mark suddenly grabbed her around the waist and he gave her a toss, but not before she got a good hold of his T-shirt. They both fell into the lake with a giant splash and flailing limbs.

Julia surfaced with a cry of indignation, while Mark was laughing heartily just a few feet away.

"I thought you needed to chill out, Juli," he teased her.

"Yes, well, I'll be lucky if I don't get pneumonia," she shot right back. "Then I'll have to call in sick, and you'll have to explain why I'm not at work."

"I would be honored," Mark said, feigning a stuffy English accent. He sounded like Sir Walter.

Floating on his back now, Mark looked as if he hadn't a care in the world. With her palm, Julia hit the water, sending a large splash in his direction. Her aim was perfect, but he just laughed, irritating Julia all the more.

"I'd like to see you explain, Mark," she huffed. "Explain about me, about our son. You, the Christian man who is supposedly *married* — which is another source of irritation for me, I'll have you know."

"Juli, I never told anyone I was married."

"You didn't have to since you insist upon wearing that cheap ring."

"Hey, it's not cheap!" Mark brought himself up and began treading water. "This wedding set cost me a lot of money!"

"Twelve years ago, you didn't have a lot of money."

Julia began swimming for shore. By now night had fallen and the air was especially cold now that she was soaking wet.

Mark swam up behind her and then they walked to shore side by side in the shallow part of the water. When they reached the small stretch of beach, he grabbed her elbow and turned her to face him.

"Juli," he said on a serious note, "about your trying to be honest with me —"

She pulled out of his grasp. "Don't worry," she told him, unable to conceal her irritation, "it won't happen again."

Chapter 14

Saturday arrived, another beautiful summer day. Mark took Jesse to ride the go-carts and, afterwards, to find a fast-food place for lunch. Julia refused the offer to join them since she was still smarting over last night's confrontation. Instead, she sipped her coffee on the back porch and read a book, trying to get her thoughts off Mark and their situation.

At last he and Jesse arrived back at the cabins around one o'clock. Almost immediately the two made their way down to the lake. Glen had consented to drive the motorboat while they water-skied.

Another barbeque was planned, but this time it would be family members only — and this included Mark, of course. It was to be a special picnic, since this was Julia's last full day up north. Tomorrow afternoon she would leave for home. But, instead of enjoying another sunny afternoon by the lake, Julia decided to stay in the cabin and cook up some homemade potato salad. It would save her mother some work since this was, after all, Caroline's vacation, too. On the other hand, staying inside the cabin was a nice way to avoid Mark, or so Julia had thought.

"What? Do I have to throw you in the lake again?"

Julia started at the sound of Mark's voice. "Didn't anyone ever tell you that it's not nice to sneak up on a person?"

"Who? Me?" Mark grinned. "I walked right through that back door, Juli — didn't even try to be quiet about it." His gaze went to the bowl of diced potatoes, mayonnaise, chopped celery and onion. "That looks good."

"I'm not done yet."

Mark took a finger full anyhow. "Aren't you coming out?" he asked, smacking his lips.

"Well, yes . . . I'll come out in a while," she stated on a note of resignation. "I just have to finish up here."

Mark leaned against the counter and, though she wasn't looking at him at the moment, she could feel the weight of his stare.

"Hey, Juli, let's be friends," he finally said.

She turned to look at him now, and he continued, "I have absolutely no intention of fighting you for custody of Jesse. I'm just sorry the thought ever entered your pretty head!"

She ignored Mark's attempted charm. "I'm sorry, too," she said stiffly. "Next time I'll keep my thoughts to myself."

Mark sighed. "Look, Juli, I want you to be honest and open with me. I really do. But it hurts me when you act as though I'm just waiting for the moment when I can ruin your life. That's so totally opposite of what I'm all about. The whole idea behind my trying to get in touch with you all these years was so that I could somehow right all the wrongs between us. Won't you just give me a chance?"

Julia considered what he said. "Do you really care about my feelings?"

"Of course I do."

She searched his face, his eyes — windows to the soul — and all she saw was sincerity. "You know what, Mark? I believe you. I really do."

He smiled broadly. "I'm glad to hear that. And as for the wedding ring, I've been wearing it for years, as I told you before. It's like a part of me, so I'm not taking it off."

Julia shrugged, turning back to her potato salad. She added some chopped green pepper, and began blending it in. "The decision is and always has been yours, Mark."

He leaned closer to her. "Aren't you even going to ask me why I'm being so stubborn about this?"

Julia stopped her stirring and looked at him.

"You've challenged me over lesser things."

She sighed impatiently. "You already told me why you're wearing that ring."

"I told you in part. You wouldn't let me finish."

She quieted. She'd let him finish today.

"It reminds me of you, Juli," Mark told her softly. "I never stopped loving you, either. I tried — just like you tried to stop loving me. It didn't work, though, did it? With either of us?"

Julia shook her head as Mark's soft voice and sweet words penetrated her heart.

She put down her spatula and wiped her hands on her apron. She considered Mark under careful scrutiny and, again, saw that light of sincerity in his blue eyes. Julia knew then that they were more than just sweet words.

"You mean it, don't you?"

"It pains me that you even have to ask, but, yes, I mean every word." He shook his head, looking troubled. "Oh, Juli . . ."

Mark hesitated for a moment, then pulled her into his arms. Julia couldn't deny the warmth of his embrace. It seemed to melt the years of loneliness in her life. Slowly, her arms went around his neck and she buried her face in his shirt. He smelled good, like the wind off the lake and the North Woods.

Mark's arms were around her waist, holding her tightly. "Juli, Juli," he murmured against her hair, "I've waited so long to hold you in my arms again . . . to kiss you . . ."

She heard his husky sigh, but instead of a kiss, Mark pushed her away slightly. "But we've got to be careful," he told her with a sudden, pleading look. "Do you understand?"

She understood completely. Their Christian testimony was at stake. Her father was watching them closely to see if all this talk about faith, love, and personal holiness was for real. And their co-workers would be watching, too.

Mark's smile broadened, and Julia decided that he looked relieved.

Reluctantly, she let her arms slide from his shoulders, and Mark's arms dropped from around her waist.

Just then Caroline entered the cabin and walked into the kitchen. She smiled happily. "How's the potato salad coming along, Juli? It was so nice of you to offer to do this for me."

"My pleasure. It's just about done."

"Tastes like it's already done to me," Mark said, snitching another finger full. This won him a smack on the hand with the spatula and Caroline chuckled.

"Oh, you two," she said, shaking her head at them. "You act as though you're the best of friends." Caroline's smile broadened. "Twelve years may have gone by, but some things never do change, do they?"

"Nope," Mark replied, looking over at Julia.

She met his meaningful gaze for a long moment before turning back to the potato salad. And she couldn't deny the burst of joy, permeating her heart of hearts.

After the morning worship service the next day, Barb and Glen made the announcement that they were staying another week.

"We'd like Jesse to stay with us," Glen

said to Julia. "You have to work all week anyway."

"Since Mark is driving back," Barb added, "we thought you could ride home with him today instead of us."

Julia looked over at her son who was frowning heavily. "Will you stay another week, Jess?"

He shook his head. "I want to go with Dad."

Mark smiled and put an arm around Jesse's chair. They were both still sitting at the kitchen table, having just finished their lunch. "Listen, Jesse," he explained, "I've got to work all week just like your mom. So, it's fishing and swimming this week for you and, boy, am I jealous!"

Jesse grinned.

"We'll come back up next weekend and get you," Mark promised. Then he looked at Julia. "How about it?"

"I'm supposed to have the pager next weekend, but I'm sure I can work something out."

Nodding, Mark looked back at his son. "We'll see you next weekend."

"I guess so." Jesse sounded doleful as he peered out at Julia. "You'll still call me every night, though, right, Mom?"

"Right."

He turned to Mark. "Will you call me, too?"

"Sure."

At last Jesse seemed pacified. He was staying.

Julia loaded her luggage into the backseat of the Impala feeling a bit melancholy. She didn't want to leave Jesse — she didn't even want to leave. This vacation had done wonders for her mind and spirit, and now it would be difficult to go back to Weakland Management and confront the daily routine.

And then, of course, there was Mark. It would be awkward to work with him, and though she loved him, she wondered if she could trust him. To Julia, trusting meant letting go and, in this case, it meant letting go of all those heart matters she had reined in so tightly, both at work and in her personal life. Could she really let them go so easily?

Julia hugged her parents good-bye, then the Frenches, and finally Jesse. "I love you." She planted a kiss on his cheek.

"Love you, too, Mom," Jesse replied automatically. "Bye, Dad." He looked up at Mark adoringly.

"Good-bye for now." Mark embraced his son, and Julia wondered if it was the first time ever. Then, in a manly effort to conceal his emotion, she watched as Mark tousled the boy's hair. "See you next week."

Julia's heart lurched as the two pulled apart. Father and son, they had missed so much of each other's life.

Mark turned toward her then, and she saw a tumult of emotions cross his face. "Ready?" he asked.

She nodded.

With family members waving good-bye, they pulled away from the cabins and drove down the gravel road.

Julia was silent for the first mile. So was Mark. In fact, they both seemed to be struggling with the same sort of things — regret from the past, apprehension for the future.

Finally, she looked over at Mark and said, "I'm really sorry that I didn't try to find you years ago and tell you about Jesse. I should have. You had every right to know about him, but I was . . . well . . ."

"Juli, don't bring that up again. The past is dead and gone. So forget it, okay?"

"No, it's not okay. The past might be dead and gone for you, but I'm still wrestling with the beast."

Silence again for the next few miles. Then, finally, it was Mark who spoke. "You know, Juli, I think that's your biggest problem. You won't let go of the past."

"My biggest problem?" she asked, lifting a brow. "You mean there are more?"

Mark glanced at her. "And you're defensive, too."

Julia swallowed a tart reply, knowing it would only prove his point. But as she stewed in silence, it occurred to her that Mark was right. She knew she wasn't "letting go." Let go, let God, she reminded herself.

Mark sighed wearily. "I suppose we're at war again, huh?"

"No," Julia replied softly. "In fact, I agree with you, Mark. You hit my problem right on the head. But, believe it or not, I'm working on it."

She chanced a look at him, saw his astonished expression and almost laughed out loud. There's quite a lot to say for blatant honesty, she thought, if it leaves Mark Henley speechless!

Two and a half hours later, they stopped for supper at a little restaurant called Buckey's, just outside of New London. It was a quaint little diner that served up family style meals, complete with homemade pie for dessert.

Then it was back on the highway.

It was after seven o'clock when Mark pulled up in front of Julia's apartment complex. "I'll help you with your luggage."

"Thanks."

She had wanted to say that it wasn't necessary for him to help her since she had been carrying her own luggage for years, but Julia was practicing the fine art of conciliation.

"Where do you want them?" he asked entering the foyer, a suitcase in each hand.

"Would you carry them upstairs?"

"Sure."

Climbing the stairs, Mark stopped just outside the living room and deposited the suitcases in the hallway which led to the two bedrooms. "Nice place," he remarked, looking around.

Julia smiled. "Thank you. It's nothing fancy, but it's home."

"It feels like a home . . . except for the weird art hanging on your walls." Mark tipped his head to one side, examining the painting over her couch. "What is this supposed to be?"

Julia laughed. "It's not supposed to be anything. It's just the colorful product of the artist's imagination."

Mark was shaking his head. "I always

think a painting is supposed to look like something. A beach, a vase of flowers, some historical building or landmark . . . something like that."

Julia said nothing but still sported a grin.

Mark turned to her then. "Guess we'll never agree on artwork."

"Guess not."

He was looking at her so intently now that Julia's pulse quickened.

"I had a great weekend," Mark said, taking a step closer.

"Me, too," Julia replied, gazing back at him and marveling at how he could affect her so.

"Well," he said, looking down at the carpet, "I'll see you tomorrow."

Julia nodded.

Mark walked down the stairs to the foyer and Julia followed. "Oh, and about to-morrow," he said, his hand on the knob of the heavy, wood-paneled front door. He looked at her with a softness in his blue eyes. Then he touched her cheek with the back of his knuckles. "Just remember I love you, okay?"

She frowned. "What do you mean? What's going to happen tomorrow?" She tried to keep the worry out of her voice.

"Juli, you're just going to have to trust

me on this one — and I mean really trust me."

She swallowed hard. "But, Mark —"

"We'll talk tomorrow, all right?"

"But —"

Leaning forward, Mark's lips touched hers ever so briefly. It was, however, long enough to cause Julia to forget her immediate thoughts.

He grinned. "Good night, Juli-bean."

After his car pulled away from the curb, Julia let out an exasperated moan. Mark had kissed her to shut her up.

Worst of all, it had worked!

Chapter 15

Monday morning's meeting was in Mark's office, since it used to be the conference room and since it was the most spacious "office" currently in the building. Mark had informed her about the meeting just before breakfast, though he wouldn't say what it was about.

Entering Mark's office now, Julia immediately noticed Bill Weakland and Jerry Fein sitting across from Mark's desk. Then she spotted another man whom she didn't recognize sitting in a chair beside Bill.

"C'mon in, Juli," Mark said, wearing a serious expression; however, there was a softer light in his eyes. "And, please, close the door."

Following Mark's instructions, Julia walked over to the vacant chair which was positioned at the foot of his desk.

Then Mark made the introductions. "You know Jerry and Bill, of course, and this is Frank Houston. He's with the FBI.

Frank . . . Julia McGowan."

The well-groomed man, dressed in a dark suit, stood politely, and Julia noticed that he wasn't very tall. "Pleased to meet you, Miss McGowan."

She nodded and shook his hand, wondering why someone from the FBI would be here at Weakland Management — and why he'd sit in on this meeting.

She looked expectantly at Mark, then at Bill.

"While Mark was browsing through your programs, Juli," Bill began, "he stumbled across something that didn't make a whole lot of sense . . . at first. He came to me with it, and I had Jerry do an audit. Our findings were shocking. Here, take a look at these."

Bill handed her a stack of green-and-white statements, and Julia looked each one over. Her trained, technical eye scanned the names, addresses, column alignments, and balances in the bottom boxes. It seemed to her that the statements had printed out just fine.

"What's the problem?" she asked at last.

"The arithmetic is the problem," Jerry Fein interjected, earning a sharp glance from Mark. He closed his mouth and sat back in his chair, folding his arms over his chest.

"Juli, the percentage that Weakland Management charges its customers in commission fees doesn't equal the amount charged on the statements." Pulling out a small calculator, Mark demonstrated his point. "The figures are off by about one and a half percent."

"Actually, they're off by a little more," Jerry said, "and it hardly seems significant. However, when you consider the millions of dollars this company invests, that extra percentage adds up to quite a tidy sum."

Julia was still peering at the statements. "How can that be? That particular software package isn't capable of what you just described."

"No, but the program you created is," Mark interjected.

Julia stared at Mark in disbelief. "The one I created . . . ?"

He nodded. "You loaded it onto my PC along with all the other programs. I found it, as Bill said, while I was 'browsing.' "

"But that's not a live program," Julia replied, referring to the one she was working on for the portfolio managers. "It's still in the developmental stages."

"I didn't know about this program," Bill said.

Julia turned to him. "I had every intention of coming to you with a software presentation, but I hadn't worked out all the bugs."

"Maybe not, but you certainly worked out a nifty way of giving yourself a little spending money," Fein stated sarcastically. "Your computer program sets up bogus accounts and then transfers money right into them."

"What?" Julia couldn't believe what she was hearing.

"Juli, watch what happens when we post the payments off these statements." Turning to the computer, Mark showed her how, instead of creating a credit on the accounts, since the statements were overcharging clients, the balances were zero. The extra funds were being automatically deposited into bogus accounts.

Julia's jaw dropped slightly.

"So what we want to know, Miss McGowan," Frank Houston said, "is to what extent you're involved."

Julia had come around to stand behind Mark so she could see the computer screen better, and she was still staring at it in awe. "I . . . I don't know anything about this."

"Come now, Julia," Bill said testily, "you wrote the software. How can you not be involved?"

After a long, pensive moment, Julia shrugged helplessly.

"Did you have a nice vacation?" Jerry Fein asked with a hint of disdain in his voice.

Julia put her hands on her hips. "I went up north, Jerry, not on a shopping spree to Paris!"

"Can you prove it?"

"That's enough," Mark told him.

Julia clenched her jaw angrily. Then she glanced at Bill Weakland who had clouds of suspicion in his eyes as he looked back at her. Seeing it, Julia's indignation turned to a heartfelt pain. *He thinks I'm stealing money from the company,* she realized. *After all my long hours and hard work . . .*

"Sit down, Juli," Mark said gently.

Still looking at Bill, she shook her head. "I think I'll go call my attorney instead."

"You need an attorney, Julia?" Bill asked sardonically.

She lifted her chin. "I do if you're going to accuse me of theft."

Mark stood. "No one is accusing anybody." He looked at Bill who dropped his gaze from Julia.

"Miss McGowan," Frank Houston began, "all accusations aside, the facts remain. Funds are being embezzled from

Weakland Management, and the perpetrator is using your computer program to do it. You are, of course, the prime suspect."

Apprehension shot through Julia as she slowly looked over at Mark. He was staring blankly at the statements on his desk with his lips pursed thoughtfully. Did he think she was guilty, too?

Then she recalled what he had said last night. *Just remember I love you.*

Yeah, right, she thought cynically. *I'll be in jail and he'll take Jesse!*

Julia entertained the thought that, perhaps, Mark had even set her up in order to take what he wanted and to get her out of his way and another blast of panic left her unable to reason.

"The idea does seem rather ludicrous, though," Houston said, and Julia momentarily wondered if she had spoken out loud. Then she realized that the man was referring to her as a suspect. "Whoever is doing the embezzling is somehow making transfers from the account here to another bank and, since one of those transactions occurred from Miss McGowan's terminal and —"

"What?" she asked incredulously.

"It's true, Juli," Mark said. "We've investigated it thoroughly. Your PC was used to make an illegal transfer. The other two were made from the CPU room. Altogether, there were three transfers made in the last two months and the dates coincide to the dates that you were on-call. Furthermore, your initials and password are all over everything."

"I don't believe it," Julia murmured.

"I guess my thoughts are," Houston continued, "that if you were going to embezzle money, Miss McGowan, you'd be intelligent enough to use someone else's PC, initials, and password and not your own." He looked around. "She's much too obvious a target."

"I agree," Mark said, but Julia couldn't bring herself to look at him. "Juli has access to everyone's passwords. Why would she use her own?"

"Perhaps because this is the very guise Juli had hoped for all along," Fein replied suggestively.

Julia glared at him for a long moment before looking over at Mark. "Why can't we trace the three money transfers?" she asked, struggling to keep her voice calm and even.

"We've tried that already," he replied. "But the accounts that received the transfers were already closed. We'll have to do a little more digging. Why don't you sit down, Juli, so we can discuss a plan of action?"

Reluctantly, she sat.

"Bill? You wanted to begin?"

He nodded. "Basically, you have two choices, Juli. You can resign from Weakland Management or you can step down from your managerial position." He glanced at Mark. "I'm in favor of terminating your employment —"

"What about my idea, Bill?" Mark interjected.

"I don't know . . ."

Julia felt sick as she thought over Bill's ultimatum. After all these years of faithful service, how could he think she'd steal money from the company?

Then, stubbornly, she made up her mind. "I'll resign, thank you very much." She stood and turned for the door.

"Hold on, Juli," Mark said, grabbing her upper arm. She shrugged out of his grasp, and he gave her a curious look. "Let's not overreact, here, all right?" He turned to Bill. "If Juli is innocent, which I know she is — which Frank thinks she is — how is her resignation going to help? Why don't we tap her resources as a programmer instead — so we can find the real culprit?"

"I don't think so." She glared at Bill, swallowing down the last of her indignation. "For years I've dedicated myself to Weakland Management," she said in a fierce but steady tone. "I've sacrificed time with my son — with my family — so that I could make sure things were running smoothly here. I've done over and above for this company, and my track record proves it! But you, Bill, are free to think what you'd like."

With that she left Mark's office, willing herself not to slam the door.

Twenty minutes later, she deposited her letter of resignation on Bill Weakland's desk. He wasn't in his office and, as she passed by, she noticed that the door to Mark's office was still closed.

Back in Information Systems, she said nothing to her employees after she telephoned for a security guard. She knew the rules stated that a guard had to watch employees, resigned or terminated, pack their things. Julia was certain that she was no exception. The security guard would also have to escort her from the building. Then, later, someone would have to come for her company PC and modem at home. It was all very humiliating.

"Your services won't be necessary after all. You may return to your own department. Thank you." Julia looked up when she heard Bill Weakland's voice. Next she watched the security guard leave her office, after which Bill closed the door.

She stopped packing her desk.

"I came to apologize," he said stiffly. "I can't deny that you have an outstanding history with Weakland Management." He took a deep breath. "I would like you to rethink your resignation. Take a couple of days if you must."

"And if I stay?"

"If you stay, you'll be offered a new position. Because of the situation, you can't run IS. Things need to change, and Mark has some very good thoughts on the subject. I think they'll work."

Julia folded her arms. "But you think I'm stealing money."

"Look, Julia, *someone* is stealing money, and if this person isn't caught soon, I could be brought up on criminal charges. As owner of Weakland Management, I could be found personally responsible for the stolen money. Fortunately, I informed the authorities before any clients filed complaints with the DA's office. But if the public finds out before we can correct the problem . . ." Bill shook his head and sighed wearily. "Reputation is everything in this business and the slightest murmur against us will be critical."

Julia chewed her lower lip thoughtfully.

"Why don't we go back upstairs and discuss this situation, and your new position, with Mark. I hired him for his ideas and he's full of them."

Julia softened, sensing that Bill was under an enormous amount of pressure. Over the years, she'd had the utmost respect for him, and it was hard to see him bowing beneath this burden.

"All right," she said at last, "I'll agree to, at least, a discussion."

She followed Bill out of her office and managed a smile for her employees. She turned to her assistant. "Angela, continue to cover for me, okay? I'll be back in a little while."

Angela nodded and the look on her face spoke of her relief. Obviously she'd sensed that something was amiss and the security officer had only confirmed it.

Julia locked her office door and then continued to follow Bill to the elevators. As she waited beside him for the car, her thoughts turned to Mark. It was most likely because of his influence that Bill apologized. In all the years she worked for him, Julia could never recall Bill Weakland apologizing to anyone — except, perhaps, an irate client.

Then she remembered back to when Mark first told her to be careful and lock up her belongings and her office door. He must have suspected that something like this was going on then, and suddenly Julia felt guilty for ever imagining Mark would set her up so she'd go to jail. How hurt he'd be if he knew that, while he had thought the best of her, she had thought the worst of him. She had accused him of everything from wanting to break her heart again to fighting her for custody of Jesse. And even with the evidence stacked against her, Mark believed she was innocent.

Julia and Bill rode the elevator in silence and then walked down the hallway to Mark's office. He smiled as they came in.

"Did things get straightened out?"

Bill nodded curtly. "Julia has agreed to hear your ideas, Mark."

"Good."

Julia gave him a smile, feeling quite humbled. Then she noticed that Jerry Fein and Frank Houston were gone. "Where are the other two?"

"They went back to work," Mark replied. "Frank said he'll check in with us in a few days." He pulled a chair over and sat down. "Ready to hear my ideas, Juli?"

"Ready as I'll ever be."

Mark grinned. "What do you think about an Operations Department?"

Julia lifted an inquiring brow. "Operations?"

Mark nodded. "It'll be a brand-new department here at Weakland Management, and you would be the one to implement it."

"What about my current department?"

"Bill can select someone else to take it over."

Julia shrugged, not exactly thrilled with the Operations idea. She thought it was something of a setback, as far as her career. Still, she understood that, in order to clear herself of any wrongdoing, she would have to accept the changes. It was either that or resign, which was still a possibility.

"Now about our new Operations Department . . ."

Julia listened for the next hour as Mark explained his ideas. The position wasn't anything she would ever apply for since there wasn't any programming involved. She would be working primarily with the hardware and only monitoring the software. She was not to work with any of the programs themselves. She could only advise from a distance.

"It's for your own protection," Mark explained.

Julia understood. If she wasn't using the computer system and the embezzling continued, she couldn't be a suspect. Furthermore, the thief wouldn't be able to use her as a cover.

"What do you say, Julia?" Bill asked.

She looked at him, then at Mark, weighing her options. She wasn't exactly strapped for cash. If she resigned, she'd have about five weeks coming in vacation pay. She had a savings account and during the summer months she wouldn't have to pay the tuition for Jesse's private Christian day school. Perhaps she and Jesse would make it until she found another place of employment.

On the other hand, she wasn't quite ready to give up her career with Weakland Management — not when Mark and Bill were offering her a chance to clear her name. Besides, she had a lot of time invested in this company.

"Juli? What do you think?" Mark widened his gaze and nodded slightly as if it was the decision he wanted her to make.

Julia smiled. "Yes, all right. I'll give it a go."

Chapter 16

"I almost had a heart attack when you told Bill Weakland off this morning!" Mark exclaimed. He collapsed onto Julia's couch with a throaty moan. "Here I had been tiptoeing around Bill, negotiating, mediating . . . and then you tell him off!"

"Well, it's not as though I planned it," Julia stated in her own defense.

Mark relented. "I know." He grinned. "You're just as sassy as they come, that's all."

Shaking her head at him, Julia smiled and set down her purse and attaché case. They had just walked in, having eaten dinner at a local Greek restaurant. "Should we call Jesse now?" she asked, taking off her red blazer and throwing it carelessly over the other end of the couch.

"Give me a few minutes . . . I'm exhausted."

Still smiling, Julia sat in the adjacent swivel-rocker. She was filled to the gills after devouring a Gyro sandwich with the works, and now she was feeling like a beached whale. But, overeating aside, the evening had been a very pleasant one.

"Thanks for dinner," Julia murmured.

"My pleasure."

A few minutes of amicable silence passed during which Julia couldn't help but consider Mark as he lay stretched out on her couch. There was a placid expression on his face — a face that was tanned with just a hint of golden stubble around his jawline and chin. A lock of blond hair had fallen rakishly onto his forehead, and his chest, beneath the light blue dress shirt and blue-and-tan speckled tie, rose and fell slowly, methodically. Then he started to snore.

"Hey! You're not falling asleep, are you?"

"No! No . . . of course not," Mark replied a little too quickly. "I'm just resting my eyes."

Julia chuckled. Who did he think he was fooling?

Then Mark cleared his throat and sat up, among the living again. His gaze met hers with blue intensity. She smiled back.

"Honestly, Juli," he sighed, "I thought you'd hate me right about now. I thought that you'd somehow blame me for what happened today. I worried that everything good between us would fall to pieces." Mark sighed once again. "I didn't sleep a wink last night."

Julia's heart went out to him, and she couldn't bring herself to confess that she'd nearly succumbed to all he had feared.

"Mark," she said softly, "I don't blame you at all. And thanks so much for believing in me. With the evidence stacked against me, you could have easily thought the worst."

He shook his head. "I could never believe the worst of you. No matter what."

Touched to the core of her being, Julia smiled. She sat there, looking at Mark, unable to speak. Then, needing something to dispel her discomfort, she stood and picked up the cordless phone. "Ready to call Jesse?"

Mark nodded and she dialed the number to her parents' cabin from memory. Jesse answered at the other end.

"Hi, Mom. I knew it was going to be you."

"Your father is here, too."

"Good. Can I talk to him?"

Feeling a tad slighted, though it was short-lived, Julia passed the telephone to Mark.

"Hi, Jesse . . ."

While Mark chatted with their son, Julia kicked off her heels and walked stocking-footed into the small kitchen. She set a kettle on the stove for some tea . . . perhaps peppermint, she decided, to help digest all that food she'd consumed.

She yawned, only half-listening to Mark answering what had to be a barrage of questions from Jesse. The water boiled and she poured it into a mug, adding a tea bag and carried it back into the living room.

"I agree, Jesse, and I think that'll probably happen someday."

Sitting, Julia wondered over Mark's grave expression. She hoped Jesse wasn't getting too personal. Perhaps she'd have to talk to him about that.

"Yes, I do, Jesse. Very much." Mark's voice was soft. Then suddenly he looked at Julia and smiled. "I'm going to hand you back to your mom, okay? Okay."

Mark shook his head, still smiling, and gave Julia the phone.

She and Jesse conversed for a few minutes and then Julia shut off the phone and set it on the coffee table.

"It rained all day up there," Mark said with a smile, "so Jesse had eight hours to . . . think."

"So I gathered."

Mark just chuckled. "The kid's a thinker, that's for sure. Must be like his mother."

Smiling, Julia took a sip of her tea but then remembered her manners. "I'm sorry, Mark, would you like a cup of tea? Or a soda? Anything?"

Mark shook his head. "No, I should be leaving."

He stood and Julia set down her mug before following him to the front door.

"What were you and Jesse talking about?" she couldn't help asking.

Mark considered her for a long moment, his lips pursed in contemplation. Finally, he said, "Jesse told me about his friend Sam and how his parents were divorced. Jesse said that Sam has to spend alternate weekends with each parent and he wondered if we were going to do that to him."

"What did you say?" Julia asked in a whispered voice.

"I told Jesse I had to talk to you." He gave her a gentle smile. "Guess you and I have a lot of talking to do."

"Yes, I suppose we do."

"When you're ready."

Julia lifted surprised brows. "When I'm ready? What do you mean?" The question wasn't defensive, just curious.

Mark chucked her under the chin. "I mean, you've got enough stress in your life right now without me adding to it. There's time ahead to make decisions. But I promise, I'll never make any unyielding demands on you regarding our son. In fact, I plan to support you . . . him. But there's time to talk about all of that."

Julia felt grateful to hear he wouldn't push her. "I appreciate your sensitivity, Mark. I really do. And, yes, we'll talk later."

He gave her an affectionate wink.

"One more thing?" she asked softly, when he opened the front door.

"Shoot."

Julia cleared her throat, forcing herself to speak of the fear that was steadily growing in her heart. "Could I go to jail? I mean, what if the embezzling stops now? What if the thief isn't ever apprehended?"

Mark was shaking his head. "You're not going to jail. I won't let that happen. Besides, Houston said that since someone has gone to a lot of trouble to steal this money, he or she is not going to give up easily."

Julia nodded thoughtfully. "The love of money is the root of all evil."

"You got it. And don't worry. I'm going to do everything in my power to protect you."

"I love you, Mark," she whispered.

"I love you, too. Ever since I was seventeen."

Julia smiled.

The following morning, Mark sent a memo to all employees, announcing the changes within the company. "Angela Davis has been promoted to the Director of Information Systems," it stated, "while Julia McGowan has been named Director of Operations, a brand-new department."

"I'm impressed, Juli," Stacie said later as she watched the mahogany "pod" being erected in the area which would house Operations. The pod was an octagonal thing that enclosed four spacious workstations. Similarly, the portfolio managers worked out of a pod since it enabled communication between them without having to leave their workstations or the happenings in the stock market.

Stacie looked at Julia. "I heard from Ken that you got a little heated at the meeting yesterday and stormed out of the office." Stacie lifted a winged brow. "They didn't give you what you wanted, so you fought to get what you deserved."

Julia frowned slightly. "That's not what happened, Stacie. It was a misunderstanding. That's all. I overreacted."

"And you got a promotion? How amazing." Her expression said she didn't believe a word of it. "If you had overreacted, Juli, we would not be standing here on the third floor this afternoon. Bill despises emotional counteractions. He's strictly business, so you must have had some leverage."

Julia turned to face her. "None, Stacie . . . except for having the Lord on my side. I suppose that's all the leverage one needs."

Stacie donned a very bored expression as she continued to watch the workers erect the pod, which was nearly finished now.

Suddenly Julia felt impulsive. "Stacie, our church has a midweek worship service every Wednesday night," she ventured carefully. She'd never asked a co-worker to church before; however, lately, Stacie seemed more like a friend than a co-worker. "Would you like to go?"

"Are you asking me out on a date?" she retorted with a teasing gleam in her eyes.

Julia bit her lip in effort not to grin, but then she gave into her feelings and laughed. Even Stacie chuckled softly.

"Oh, maybe I'll think about it," she said at last.

Julia nodded, glad that Stacie hadn't refused her offer of the worship service altogether.

However, refusing Ken's flirtations was a-whole-nother story. He walked over to Juli's area every chance he got, trying to engage her in conversation, which, of course, didn't sit well with Mark.

Then, on Wednesday morning, a giant bunch of long-stemmed red roses was delivered to Julia's workstation. She couldn't help but smile when the flowers arrived . . . until she read the card: *Congratulations, Julia, and please have dinner with me tonight. Love, Ken.*

She sighed, not even chancing a look in the direction of the portfolio managers' area. Why was Ken pursuing her?

Glancing in the other direction, Julia spotted Mark standing in his doorway. His arms folded in front of him, he was leaning casually against the doorframe, but it was his probing regard that unnerved Julia. He obviously saw the roses. And he was angry.

She shrugged helplessly, and Mark turned back into his office.

Oh, brother! she thought dryly. *The testosterone level up here is going to kill me!*

Later, she ventured into Mark's office,

closing the door behind her. "Have a minute?"

"A minute." He didn't even look up from the papers on his desk.

Julia cleared her throat. "You're angry with me, Mark. I can tell. But it's not my fault that Ken keeps pestering me. And, if it's any consolation, I'm planning to return his roses and let him know I'm not interested in him, his flowers, or his dinner invitations."

Mark looked at her, pursing his lips in thought. "It's about time. Why didn't you do that sooner?"

Julia shrugged. "I thought he'd lose interest in me when he found out about Jesse, so I figured there was no need to say anything."

Mark softened his expression. "Look, I'm sorry, Juli. I'm struggling with jealousy — it's a real demon. What can I say?"

"Say you'll conquer it," she retorted.

He nodded reluctantly. "Easier said than done, but . . . I'll work on it."

"Good."

Mark gave her a helpless shrug.

Leaving his office, Julia had one more piece of evidence that Mark really did love her. His act of jealousy just now seemed to etch his words of love upon her heart.

After all, Mark wouldn't be jealous if he didn't really care.

But did he care enough? Did he love her enough to last a lifetime? Or would he change his mind again?

Trust, the Lord's voice seemed to whisper in Julia's ear.

I'm trying, her heart seemed to reply.

Chapter 17

Julia could hardly believe it. She wanted to pinch herself to be sure it was true. Here she was, sitting in a pew with Mark on her left side and Stacie Rollins on her right. If someone would have predicted this very moment a month ago, Julia would have thought the person was crazy, to say the least. Yet, here they were. Mark, back in her life after twelve years and Stacie, sitting beside her in . . . in church!

But God's timing is always perfect, Julia reminded herself. God knew the precise timing of her reunion with Mark — a time when she would accept his apology, forgive and go on, even though she and Mark still seemed to have unfinished business between them. But God was bigger than unfinished business.

And God knew the exact worship service Stacie needed to attend.

The latter seemed so obvious, since the testimonies given were poignant illustrations of God's mercy and grace. Those who stood and shared their stories described how they had been delivered from backgrounds that included marital problems, drug abuse, immorality, alcoholism and more. Furthermore, before the service had even begun, Mark and Julia had told Stacie about their pasts, God's grace, and deliverance in their lives . . . and then they told her about Jesse. Surprisingly, Stacie wasn't shocked or judgmental, but awed.

Glancing to her right now, Julia noticed that Stacie was sitting straight and still, hardly breathing, it seemed, as she listened intently. These testimonies were for her.

Except Julia could not deny the affect of these testimonies in her own heart tonight as well. That these fellow believers spoke about their painful pasts so candidly amazed her. It was obvious that they had truly been set free. And it seemed that, while Julia had tried to run from her past, those giving testimonies had allowed God to use theirs to reach others. After all, one couldn't have a present or future without a past — and look how her past had touched Stacie's heart!

Lord, I was wrong, she silently prayed, her eyes closed reverently. *I should have given my past to You a long time ago. I should have given You my hurt, my loneliness, my insecurities, my fears. Just like my career, I thought I could control my personal life, too. But I can't. And I can't change the past, either, but I can take care for the future. I can give it all to You. It's Yours anyway. My ambition, my heart . . . my life.*

When Julia opened her eyes, an errant tear fell onto her cheek. She didn't even bother to wipe it away. This, she decided, was a time to be honest before both God and man.

It occurred to her, then, that sitting beside her, were two people who represented her past and present. Mark and Stacie, even though Mark represented a little of both. And, in her heart, Jesus Christ held her future.

The pastor came up and stood at the pulpit. He delivered a brief message and then called for an invitation. Those who had made decisions were invited to share them, while those who needed salvation were urged to come and get that matter settled once and for all.

Since Stacie didn't appear to want to go forward, Julia went by herself. She knelt at the altar, silently rededicating her life to the Lord. Then she filled out a decision card — something she had always been too prideful or too stubborn to do before.

When she returned to the pew, Stacie was gone.

"Did she leave?" Julia asked, concerned.

Mark shook his head and pointed to the other end of the pew, where Stacie sat with a man who looked "thirty-something." He was obviously pointing out the way of salvation to Stacie from the open Bible in his lap.

"I've been praying for her," Mark said.

Julia nodded. She had been praying, too.

When the service ended, Julia and Mark walked out into the lobby where they stood around, chatting with other believers and waiting for Stacie.

Once the crowd thinned, Mark turned to her. "You know, I was really impressed by your decision tonight, Juli. Good for you."

She smiled. "I've never gone forward before," she confessed. "It seemed disconcerting to have something so personal read out loud to the entire congregation. But I had left my first love, Mark, and now I've come back to Him. My public profession tonight was like spiritual cement, sealing my relationship with Christ."

"That's wonderful."

Stacie finally emerged. The same gentleman who had counseled her walked beside her. When they reached Mark and Juli, Stacie made the appropriate introductions.

"Tell your friends what happened tonight," the man prompted. He had been introduced as Dr. Ryan Carlson. He was a nice-looking man with an easy smile.

Stacie seemed a little embarrassed, however. "I prayed," she announced. "I believe . . . well, I believe what Ryan showed me in the Bible tonight . . . about Christ. I believe it."

Ryan was grinning from ear to ear. "You got saved, Stacie."

"Right. That's what it's called. Saved."

Mark chuckled joyfully as Julia hugged Stacie. "We're sisters in Christ now," she whispered.

Again, Stacie looked chagrined, and Julia recalled how overwhelmed she had felt as a new believer.

"Well, I've got to be on my way," Ryan said, shaking hands with Mark. He turned to Stacie. "I'll look forward to seeing you on Sunday. I hope you'll come."

Stacie's face turned as pink as a tea rose. Then she nodded a reply to Ryan while Julia had to force herself not to gape at the sight. Stacie Rollins? The sophisticated blond from Customer Service, blushing?

Julia turned and looked up at Mark who seemed quite amused.

After Ryan departed, the three of them ambled out into the parking lot.

"I guess there are some decent single men left in the world," Stacie remarked, speaking of Ryan. She glanced at Mark. "No offense, but up until tonight, I thought you were married."

"No, I'm not married."

Mark looked over Stacie's head and met Julia's gaze in a meaningful way — except Julia wasn't sure what the meaning was. His eyes may have said, "I'll never get married as long as I live!" Or they may have implied that Mark intended to marry her . . . .

Lord, You're in control, Julia prayed silently. *I gave my future to You and I won't take it back!*

The next couple of days passed quickly for Julia. At work she stayed busy interviewing applicants for the three Operations positions. Internal applicants were given first priority, but only a handful had expressed interest.

"Here are the last of the interviews, Juli," a young woman said, handing her a printed sheet of paper. "You can begin interviewing outside candidates next week."

"Thanks." Julia paused. "You're Darlene, right?"

The woman nodded.

"I thought so. We haven't formally met, but I understand you're developing the Human Resources Department."

Darlene nodded again and managed a tired-looking grin. "I think I bit off more than I can chew."

"I know how you feel!"

They chuckled together, then Darlene left for her own department.

Later that Friday afternoon, Julia spotted Ken entering Mark's office. He closed the door behind him, and Julia glanced at her wristwatch in dismay. It was four-fifteen and she and Mark had decided to leave Weakland Management precisely at five o'clock so they could get up to Minoqua before midnight. Jesse would no doubt be waiting for them.

Five o'clock came and went, and Julia left a telephone voice-mail message for Mark, saying that she would wait for him at her apartment. He finally showed up at six-thirty.

"What in the world . . . ?"

"Sorry, Juli."

She let him into the front hallway where her suitcase stood. "Is everything all right?"

Mark nodded. "I'll tell you all about it on the way up north."

He picked up her suitcase and Julia followed him outside, locking her front door behind them.

"Well, as you probably guessed," Mark began as he pulled onto the expressway, "Ken and I had a long talk today. He gave me some song and dance about being misunderstood. The Paxton account was only one of those 'misunderstandings.' There are others, but I'm not free to discuss them at this time."

"Okay. But . . . you don't believe what Ken told you this afternoon?"

"I don't know, Juli. There's just something about that guy that makes my skin crawl."

"You're not still jealous, are you?"

Mark sighed. "I don't think so. I think I'm confident enough about where I stand with you now."

Julia smiled at his reply. Then, seriously, she said, "I think Ken is a workaholic who's hurting and needs the Lord desperately."

"Oh, yeah? And you know what you are?"

With raised brows she turned to him. "What am I?"

"You're a bleeding heart, that's what. I'll bet you'd bring home every stray dog and cat in the neighborhood if your landlord allowed it."

"I would not!" Julia retorted. She mulled over the comment and shifted uncomfortably. "Well, maybe not every stray dog or cat . . ."

"Aha! So you admit it!"

"Sort of," Julia said on a defensive note.

"Man, have I been going about this all wrong," Mark muttered.

"What do you mean? Going about what all wrong?"

"You. I should have gotten you to feel sorry for me, and then I would have had your bleeding heart right in the palm of my hand."

Julia huffed. "Fat chance."

Mark feigned an expression of pure affliction. "Oh, Juli, I've had a tragic life . . ."

"Oh, quiet."

"I've been used and abused . . ."

"With good reason," she teased.

"My parents never understood me. My friends have forsaken me. Even my dog doesn't like me."

"You don't have a dog."

243

"That's because he ran away," Mark improvised. "It was very traumatic."

"I'm sure it was, you poor thing," she crooned dramatically.

"Are you feeling sorry for me yet?"

"Absolutely," Julia replied facetiously. Then she added, "Not!"

"Well, then I'll have to lay it on heavier." Mark cleared his throat. "Oh, Juli," he began again, "my heart is crushed. I'm . . . I'm just a bug on the windshield of life."

Julia laughed. "That's pathetic, Mark!"

He sobered. "Yeah, I know, but it's timely." Manipulating the windshield wash and wipers, Mark cleared his view. "Ah, that's better." He smiled.

Julia just shook her head at him, still chuckling at his shenanigans.

Chapter 18

The following Sunday night Julia stood beside her son, helping him unpack from his two weeks up north. This past weekend had gone much like the weekend before. Sunshine, blue skies, and a crystal-clear lake for swimming, fishing, and water-skiing. And, if it were possible, Julia thought she'd fallen even more in love with Mark Henley.

"Hey, Mom?" Jesse began as he put a clean shirt away in his dresser drawer. "Do you think you'd ever marry Dad?"

Julia stopped her unpacking. "Why do you ask?"

Jesse shrugged. "Just wondering."

She smiled. "Well, first of all, your dad would have to ask me to marry him, and since that hasn't happened yet, we shouldn't even speculate on the 'what ifs.'"

"But —"

"Now, Jesse, you heard what I said."

"But let's pretend Dad asked you. Would you marry him?"

Julia chewed her lower lip in momentary thought. "Jesse, I love your father. I really do. But let's see what the Lord does with the future."

"If you love him, you should marry him," Jesse muttered irritably.

"But I can't marry him if he hasn't asked me," Julia replied.

"But if he did — would you?"

"Oh, Jesse . . ." Julia sat down on the twin-size bed covered with a blue bedspread with baseball players scattered about. The question of marrying Mark had entered her head dozens of times, but always a bit of fear put a check in her heart when she remembered how he had left her at the altar. But that was more than a decade ago and the past belonged to God to use as He saw fit. And she did love Mark. She had been dreaming of spending the rest of her life with him, as his wife.

Looking at her son, his wondering blue eyes staring back at her, Julia smiled. "You know, Jess, if your dad asked me to marry him, I'd probably say . . ." She paused just to tease him.

"What would you say?"

"I'd say . . ."

"What!"

"I'd say . . . yes!"

"Hooray!" Jesse said, throwing a sweat shirt into the air.

Julia stood and caught it. Then she pointed a warning at her son. "But your dad hasn't asked, and I don't think either of us should get our hopes up. Okay? I mean, what if your dad doesn't want to get married?"

"Oh, he does."

Jesse suddenly looked like the Cheshire cat and Julia narrowed her gaze. "Okay. Spit it out. What do you know?"

"I can't tell," Jesse said. "I promised."

Julia rolled her eyes. "Then you shouldn't have said anything, Jesse, because now I'm going to be nervous."

"Don't be nervous, Mom," Jesse coached her. "Just say yes."

Julia lifted a brow. "So he's going to pop the question, huh? When?"

"I don't know. Dad said he had to wait for the perfect moment."

Julia handed the boy a few more articles of clothing to put into his dresser.

"Dad says he wants us to be a real family. That's what I want, too. And I think he'll be a good dad, once he gets the hang of it."

Julia chuckled softly. "Well, I just hope you thanked your father for those cleats he bought you on the way home today."

"I did. They're the best, aren't they?"

"For that price, they'd better be!" Julia mumbled. She had told Mark not to spend so much money on shoes that would most likely be wrecked by August, but since Jesse had wanted them so badly, he gave in.

With the unpacking finished, Julia closed the suitcase and then left the bedroom so Jesse could change into his pajamas. Once he was dressed for bed, Julia tucked him in, kissing his forehead and wishing him a good night.

Undressing in her own bedroom now, Julia thought over the conversation she and Jesse had about Mark's alleged impending marriage proposal. The idea of planning a wedding sent terrors through Julia.

Oh, Lord, she whispered, *why can't I get over this? Mark left me once, but he wouldn't do it again. He's a different person altogether . . .*

Besides, Mark wouldn't dare leave me twice. My father would have him flogged!

But even with that bit of "assurance," Julia couldn't seem to find peace in accepting Mark's marriage proposal.

Then she laughed at her presumption: Mark hadn't even asked her! What was she thinking?

Forgive me, Lord, for running ahead of You again . . .

The next morning, Julia took her habitual run. The day was bright and sunny, but hot and humid. The air was thick, making Julia's exercise more of an effort than usual. Re-entering her apartment then, she praised God for central air conditioning.

"Jesse, time to get up," Julia called in the direction of his bedroom.

"I'm up. I'm up."

She smiled. His voice didn't sound "up." It sounded sleepy.

"Your vacation is over," she told Jesse as they walked to the car later. "It's back to reality for you, which means you're up and dressed and then we're both out of the apartment by seven-thirty."

"You don't have to remind me." Her soon-to-be twelve year old seemed crabby this morning.

"Have fun at practice," Julia told him, leaving him off at the Frenches' house.

"Bye, Mom," he muttered.

At work, Julia was surprised to discover that her son wasn't the only crab this morning. The tension was so thick on the third floor that finally Julia decided to see

249

how Angela was doing with her reorganizing of IS. On the way over, she met Stacie.

"What's the matter, Juli," Stacie cooed in a sarcastic manner. "Can't take it up there with the big boys?"

"You got that right."

Stacie laughed at the admission. Then, more seriously, she asked, "Is it really that bad up there?"

Julia nodded. "It's a big trading day."

"Wonderful. I hope we make lots of money!"

Julia headed for Information Systems with Stacie walking beside her.

"I went to church yesterday," she said, looking somewhat abashed. "I had lunch with Ryan afterwards."

"Oh?"

"Yes. I never knew a Christian man could be so charming and so polite at the same time. And a doctor . . . I think I'm in love!"

Stacie laughed, and Julia smiled as they parted at the door of IS. Walking to the back of the department, Julia entered the rearranged office. Angela had moved the desk and the credenza.

"This looks nice," Juli remarked.

Angela smiled slightly. "I decided on a

change. Actually, lots of changes . . . but some I don't have a say in."

"Mark?"

"Bingo. And he'll be here shortly. This is our department's week with him. Remember?"

Julia couldn't help but grin. "Sorry I won't be here to help," she teased.

Angela cocked a brow. "We know where to find you."

They shared a laugh.

Julia looked down at Angela's desk, then, and spotted two stacks of green-and-white statements. "What are these doing here?"

"Mark gave them to me. I'm supposed to key-in the correct payments which leave a credit balance on each account. Then Weakland Management has to reimburse the clients."

Julia nodded ruefully.

"There must have been a problem with the computer program, right?" Angela's large, brown-eyed gaze searched Julia's face.

"There was a big problem, Angela. Didn't Mark tell you about it?"

"Some . . . which, uhm, program was it?"

"A new one I was working on. It wasn't even a live program, or so I thought.

Someone tampered with it. He or she interfaced it with the current portfolio managers' program and did some embezzling."

Angela paled visibly. "How . . . how was that discovered?"

"Mark found it."

"I see." Angela turned suddenly pensive.

"Don't worry," Julia assured her, "this isn't going to affect your taking over Information Systems."

"But that's why you got moved?"

Julia nodded. "That news is just between you and me, Angie, okay? I thought you should know since you're taking over here. They wouldn't have given you the job if they didn't trust you."

She nodded. But then her gaze darkened and a troubled look crossed her features.

"What is it, Angela?"

She shrugged.

"Tell me." It was more a gentle prompting than a command.

Angela sighed. "It's our business consultant . . . it's Mark."

"What about him?"

"Well, I walked in on him rummaging through your desk. It was the Saturday after his first week here. I had left my wallet in my desk drawer and, since I was having breakfast with friends, I needed to stop by Weakland Management and get it. It was only seven-thirty in the morning, but there he was, shuffling through all your files and anything else you might have had in there."

"Why didn't you tell me this sooner?" Julia asked.

"I was afraid. He saw me. I feared for my job. I mean, there were rumors flying that half of Weakland's employees were going to get the ax. But when nothing happened, I began to relax . . . except it's always bothered me. And now, you say, he's the one who found the embezzling program . . ."

"But it's been going on for months," Julia countered. "Mark couldn't be involved, if that's what you mean."

Angela shrugged. "I heard he did off-site work for Bill before coming here. I suppose he could have used a modem —"

"Highly unlikely."

"But not impossible."

Folding her arms in front of her, Julia wondered what this meant. She suspected Mark's "rummaging" through her office was just all part of that "investigation" he had mentioned last Monday. One illegal money transfer, after all, had been made from her PC.

Julia shrugged it off. "Don't lose any

sleep over it, Angela. Whoever stole the money will be discovered sooner or later."

"Okay, if you say so," she said waveringly.

Julia smiled more confidently than she felt. "I'd better get back to work, Angie. See you later."

Julia returned to the third floor about a half hour after she'd left. The tension hadn't lessened, but she did her best to ignore it and went about her own business. She did her best to discount Angela's news, too; however, it sat in her mind, lurking like a dark shadow that she couldn't shake.

Mark, she noticed, was out of his office almost all day, consulting with the IS department. But, finally, Julia got a chance to speak with him at the end of the afternoon when he ambled over to "check in."

"Everything going all right?" he asked, peering over the side of the workstation.

"Well . . ." *Now is not the time to discuss what Angela told me,* she decided. "Yes, everything is fine," she finally replied with a smile. "I hired two of my three employees today."

Mark looked surprised. "You don't waste any time, do you?"

She laughed and shook her head.

"They're the ones for the job. I just know it."

He smiled and glanced at his wristwatch. "I'd like to take Jesse to a baseball game tonight," he said, changing the subject. "Want to come along?"

"What time?"

"Oh . . ." He looked at his watch again. "As soon as we can change clothes and pick him up at Barb and Glen's. We can grab supper at the stadium." He grinned. "I just love those stadium hot dogs. They just have that . . . taste, you know?"

Julia grimaced. "I don't know about the hot dogs, but Jess will love going to the baseball game tonight."

"You, too?"

She grinned. "Only if I can have a cheeseburger."

Mark chuckled. "I guess we can make an exception for you. I'll meet you over at Barb and Glen's place, okay?"

Julia nodded and Mark walked back to his office.

"You're awfully quiet tonight," Mark said as they sat in the bleachers, watching the Milwaukee Brewers.

"It was that hot dog!" Julia declared teasingly. "I shouldn't have listened to you."

"I enjoyed every bite."

"I know. You ate four." Julia shook her head. "So did Jesse . . . and if he gets sick in the middle of the night tonight, I'm calling you."

"I won't get sick!" Jesse said from on the other side of Mark.

Julia smiled and turned back to the game. She hoped her feelings of discomfort didn't show — her true reason for being especially quiet tonight. The fact was, Angela's news had begun to trouble Julia greatly, and now she wasn't sure what to do. If she mentioned it to Mark, would he take offense? Julia didn't want that. She and Mark had come so far.

Forcing her disturbing thoughts aside, Julia decided all she could do was try to enjoy the rest of the evening.

The game ended and the crowd dispersed to the parking lot. From there it was slow going until Mark accelerated onto the expressway. Jesse talked most of the way home, comparing his baseball teammates with the Brewers.

"And Sam can hit a ball as good as Cirello, but I can pitch like Cal Eldred."

"Who?" Mark teased him. "I'm a White Sox fan, Jess."

"Oh no." Jesse turned around and

looked at Julia who had graciously volunteered to sit in the backseat. "Did you hear that, Mom? He's a Chicago fan!"

"Mark, how could you?" Julia said, shaking her head in mock disappointment. "Well, don't worry, Jess, we'll convert him this summer."

"You think so?" Mark commented. "I don't know . . ."

The amiable banter continued until Mark parked his car in front of Julia and Jesse's apartment complex.

"Thanks, Dad," Jesse said as he opened the car door and jumped out. Then he ran to the front door.

"There are days," Julia told Mark, "when Jesse goes to bed with more energy than I wake up with."

"I believe it."

Mark walked her to the front door where Jesse stood waiting.

"Would you like to come in for a while?" Julia asked, fishing in her purse for her keys.

"No, I've got to be on my way."

"Will you come to my first baseball game on Friday night?" Jesse asked Mark.

"You bet."

Julia smiled. "Good night, Mark, and thanks."

"Sure. See you tomorrow, Juli . . . 'night, Jess."

"Hey, aren't you guys even gonna kiss? Sam's mom kisses her boyfriend when they —"

"Get yourself in the house," Julia said on a note of admonishment as her cheeks warmed with embarrassment.

She glanced at Mark who looked thoroughly amused. He did, however, have the good grace to turn and walk back to his car. "Before I get to thinking too hard about Jesse's question," he called over his shoulder. "I might want to do something about it then."

Julia smiled. "Good night."

Chapter 19

The rest of the week passed quickly for Julia. She stayed busy organizing her new department. Two employees were scheduled to start next week and the third employee would begin the week after that.

With one situation taken care of, Julia went onto the next. She wrote and assembled a training manual since she had been allowed a word processing program on her PC. Much of the information she used had belonged to the original manual in the IS, so Julia found herself in Angela's department on several occasions, searching for things she'd left behind. Angela didn't seem to mind her presence, though she was distant to the point of being unfriendly. However, Julia was relieved when Angela didn't say another word against Mark. She had all but convinced herself that it was a misunderstanding on Angela's part and, slowly, Julia forgot about the incident.

The following Monday, Julia glanced at her wristwatch. Four-thirty. She stifled another yawn and looked over at her two new employees. They were browsing through the training manuals. Julia had decided to give them a break for the last half-hour of the day. It had been a busy one, but both employees would be outstanding team players. Julia could tell already. They were perfect for the job.

But am I? she couldn't help wondering.

It occurred to Julia today as she began training the new employees that, once they knew what they were doing, she wouldn't have anything to do. The thought of growing bored and useless wasn't appealing in the least.

At five o'clock, the employees left with a hearty "See you tomorrow!" Julia smiled and nodded. She felt exhausted. Looking across the way at Mark's office, she smiled as he waved her over.

"Tough day?" he asked as she walked in.

"Sort of," Julia replied. "I didn't sleep well last night."

Mark frowned, looking concerned. "Why not?"

She shrugged. How could she tell him that she hated her new job?

"You weren't worrying about things here

at work, were you?"

Julia shrugged once more.

"Well, you should be!" Jerry Fein cut in, entering the office unannounced. He dropped a pile of invoices on Mark's desk. "Anyone else, Juli, would have been out on her ear. Proof or inconclusive proof . . . doesn't matter. You're a suspect in this embezzling thing — your job should have been terminated." Jerry narrowed his gaze. "But since you and our business consultant are so friendly, you get to keep your job. You even got a promotion . . . sort of." He smirked.

"Can it, Fein," Mark said, seemingly unaffected. "Now what's all this that you dumped on my desk?"

As Jerry explained about the corrected invoices, Julia had to swallow down her tears of indignation. She was innocent. Jerry had no right speaking to her that way! And yet, something inside Julia wondered if he wasn't right. Bill treated her differently now, as though he didn't trust her anymore. The light of respect was no longer in his eyes when he spoke to her. Was Jerry Fein just crass enough to speak what Bill really thought of her?

Turning, Julia left Mark's office, packed her things and headed for the elevator. As she glanced across the way, she watched Mark's office door close — with Jerry Fein still inside. Part of her hoped Mark would defend her, but the other part thought that, perhaps it really didn't matter. How could she work at Weakland Management when its President and CEO didn't trust her?

Julia climbed into her car and drove out of the parking lot. Heading for the Frenches' place, where she'd pick up Jesse, she couldn't help but rehash the situation in her head. Trust was essential to any working relationship. The give and take was disproportionate if the element of trust was missing.

Then suddenly Julia realized that her thoughts on professional trust could well be applied to personal relationships, too. Trust. Wasn't it the key to salvation? Trusting in the shed blood of Jesus Christ instead of oneself or one's religious works? And in friendships trust was an awesome factor. What would she have done if Barb and Glen hadn't been trustworthy? And her parents, her brothers . . . Jesse.

"And Mark," Julia said aloud as she pulled into the Frenches' driveway. Jesse and his friend Sam were playing basketball. "How can I claim to be in love with him and still not trust him completely?"

Getting out of the car, Julia smiled a hello to the boys before walking into the house. Barb was cooking something that smelled delicious.

"You look beat!" Barb exclaimed when Julia entered the kitchen.

"Thanks a lot," she quipped.

Barb chuckled. "Oh, you know what I mean, honey. You look so tired . . . want to lie down and rest before supper?"

Julia shook her head. "I've got too much on my mind to lie down and rest. What are you making, anyway?"

"Glen is grilling hamburgers and I'm creating a pasta salad."

"What smells so good?"

"Probably my rhubarb squares in the oven."

Julia's mouth was watering already.

"As soon as Mark shows up, we'll eat."

Julia nodded. Lately it seemed Mark was over here as much as she was, and she couldn't say she minded it, either.

"Hey, Barb, do you . . . well, do you trust Mark?"

"Well, sure I do." Barb frowned. "Don't you?"

Julia momentarily chewed her lower lip. "I want to. I guess I'm just afraid to let go and trust this thing between us now."

Barb smiled in a motherly way. "Mark is a wonderful man, honey, and he loves you very much. Why, it thrills my heart every time I see the way he looks at you."

Julia's heart swelled with emotion. It was a joy to hear that from Barb. It was like affirmation from above.

Dinner was ready at last and Mark walked in with Jesse. He had been playing basketball with the kids in the driveway, suit and tie and all.

"Are we still going to the State Fair tonight?" Jesse asked, biting into a hamburger which was oozing with ketchup.

Mark looked at Julia. "Are we still going?"

She shook her head apologetically. "I'm exhausted. But you two can go."

"Can Sam come along, Dad?"

Julia saw Mark's expression register the disappointment he felt; however, he recovered and told Jesse to bring his friend.

"I'm sorry, Mark," she told him later. Jesse and Sam were already in his car waiting for him. "I'm just so tired that I don't feel like walking around the fairgrounds tonight."

He smiled. "That's all right. We'll just have to go again." With a chuckle, he added, "I don't think Jesse will mind that a bit."

"No, I'm sure he won't."

Mark climbed into his car. "I'll have Jesse home by ten o'clock."

"Aw, that's too early!" the boy exclaimed.

"Not for me, it isn't," Mark replied, grinning. "I've got to get up early tomorrow."

"So do I," Jesse countered.

"Yeah, but you have more energy than I do." Mark and Julia exchanged amused glances.

"Have fun, you guys. I'll see you at home."

She waved them off and walked back into the house. Gathering her things, she told Barb and Glen good-night. On the way out, however, she decided to grab the want ads. Just for a look.

"Can I take some of your Sunday newspaper?" she asked Glen.

"Sure. It's still on the table in the TV room."

Julia entered the room. It was decorated with a masculine touch, from the paintings of hunters on horseback, which hung on the dark paneling, to the sculptured carpet in various shades of brown. The tan, woven-fabric of the couch was worn, but still comfortable. It had once been in the living room until Barb insisted on new furniture. A large-screen TV and entertainment center had been placed against an adjacent wall and a gun case stood in the corner. This was Glen's favorite room while Barb enjoyed her sewing area in a finished section of the basement.

Julia smiled. The Frenches loved each other, but desired their own "space" too. *I wonder if Mark would want a room like this,* she mused. She couldn't seem to help it. And then she imagined father and son watching baseball games together, and football games while she baked cookies with their daughter.

Julia shook herself. *I'm getting delirious.*

However, Julia couldn't deny that part of her found the idea of home and family — having more babies — quite appealing. On the other hand, until Mark proposed, her dreams were about as attainable as catching a falling star.

Looking through the newspapers now, scattered across the coffee table, Julia found the employment section and folded it under her arm. She hadn't paged through this part of the newspaper in years — not since before she'd been hired at Weakland Management. She had always thought she'd stay with the company forever. There had been security in that idea, but no more. The Lord was her security now. She clearly saw how wrong she'd been to give her heart to her career.

Once Julia got home, she changed clothes, pulling on a "skort" which was a combination of a skirt and shorts all in one. Next she pulled on a matching T-shirt. Folding her long, tanned legs beneath her, she sat on the couch and paged through the employment section. Much to Julia's amazement, there were plenty of opportunities for which she was qualified. Getting up from the couch, she found paper and pencil and began writing down names and addresses of companies in the Milwaukee area. She'd update her resumé and send it out.

Julia was still at her task when Mark and Jesse showed up.

"Hey, Mom, look what I won!" Jesse burst into the living room, carrying a large stuffed panda bear.

"Goodness! Do people really win those things?" Julia smiled at her son, then at Mark. "I always thought those games at the midway were big rackets and that no one ever won the nice prizes."

"Well, I won . . . with Dad's help."

Mark grinned. "It was a basketball game."

"Good thing we were practicing before we went to the fair?"

"Good thing," Mark agreed. Then he spotted the want ads and Julia's notes spread all over the couch. He frowned. "What's all this?"

Julia paused, not wanting to discuss it in front of Jesse. "Time to hit the shower, Son."

"But, Mom —"

"Don't argue," Julia warned him.

Looking like a puppy with his tail between his legs, Jesse moped all the way down the hallway. Then Julia turned to face Mark.

"I was just looking . . . trying to get a feel for what kind of career opportunities are out there."

Mark regarded her through a narrowed gaze. "Why? Because of Jerry Fein's thoughtless remark this afternoon?"

Julia shrugged. "That's part of it — maybe even most of it."

"I didn't think it bothered you," Mark said softly. "You handled it well in my office, and you didn't seem upset tonight."

Swallowing the sudden urge to cry, Julia

forced herself to say, "I hate to admit it, but I think Jerry was right. Anyone else in my situation would have been fired."

Mark was shaking his head. "Not necessarily. It's a judgment call. Each situation is unique, and Fein had no right to make a blanket statement like the one he made today. Forget it, Juli. Don't let it get to you . . . oh, and don't cry . . ."

Julia swiped at the errant tear as Mark pulled her into his arms.

"I'm sorry he hurt you," Mark whispered against her ear. "But he's not right. Bill made the decision to put you in charge of Operations, I merely suggested the idea."

"But he wanted to fire me," Julia sniffled against his shoulder. "Bill admitted it."

"Well, sure . . . at first. He was angry." Mark gently pushed her from him, holding her by the shoulders at arm's distance. "One of Bill's employees is stealing money from his clients, Juli. Can you blame Bill for being upset?"

"I don't blame him, but I can't make him trust me either. I'm the prime suspect. You heard Frank Houston."

Julia pulled out of Mark's grasp. Walking over to the windows, she peered out onto the well-lit tennis courts. "Besides," she added, "I don't like my job anymore."

"Why's that?" Mark's tone indicated his surprise at her statement.

She turned back to face him. "I'm a programmer, Mark, but I'm not allowed access to the computer system because Bill doesn't trust me. Once my employees are trained, which won't be long, I'm not going to have anything to do."

"In a company that size, there's always something to do."

"Secretarial stuff, I imagine. But I don't want to be a secretary. I'm a computer programmer."

Looking pensive, Mark picked up one of Julia's notes. He read it over before bringing his blue-eyed gaze back to her. "It won't be difficult for you to find another place of employment," he said at last. "You're intelligent and a conscientious worker. You're organized and you carry yourself in a professional manner."

"Thanks," she said skeptically as Mark walked slowly toward her.

"But will you put off this job hunt for a while longer?"

"Why?"

"Because I'm asking you to."

Julia lifted her chin stubbornly. "You'll have to come up with a better reason. I'm sorry, but this is my future we're discussing. With God's help, I want to map it out, whether it means staying at Weakland Management or not."

"And how will it look if you quit now? Frank Houston said that if our embezzler even senses that we're onto him . . . or her, he or she will most likely quit."

Julia frowned. "I didn't think about that."

"Hang in there, Juli, all right? For just a while longer? Let's ask God to bring this sin to the surface. Then the thief will be apprehended and your name will be cleared."

"And that will be great, but I still won't like my job in Operations any better."

"One step at a time." Then he chuckled at her sigh of impatience. "Waiting isn't easy, is it? When I first found out where you were living and that I had a son, I wanted to jump the first airplane heading in this direction. Twice I even made weekend reservations, but each time God put an undeniable check in my heart. He didn't want me to go. It wasn't His time yet. And now I'm so glad I waited."

Mark took both her hands in his. "This will work out too, Juli. You'll see." Then suddenly he snapped his fingers with an idea. "I know. We'll talk about all this job business tomorrow night. Let's go out to dinner. Just you and me. A nice place. Fancy. Romantic . . ."

Julia immediately knew what was coming. A marriage proposal . . . just like Jesse had said. She wanted to smile and cringe at the same time. On one hand, she loved Mark and wanted to marry him, but, on the other, she knew what it meant to have a "check in her heart" because it was there in her heart right now. If only she could be sure that Mark wouldn't change his mind again. If only she could be guaranteed somehow that he'd never leave her behind.

"What do you say, Juli? Is tomorrow night okay?"

At last she nodded, unsure if she could speak.

Then, as she walked Mark to the door, Julia decided that, proposal or no proposal, she needed to be honest with him tomorrow night. No more walls for self-protection. She didn't need them; she had the Lord.

"G'night, Juli," Mark said, kissing her cheek softly. He paused before adding a whispered, "I love you."

Looking into his eyes, so blue and sincere, Julia smiled.

Chapter 20

"The next screen gives you the client's past history with us," Julia explained, sitting in between her department's two new employees. Amazingly, she had been given permission to acclimate them on various programs, even though they'd be working mostly with the hardware. "Now, the next screen —"

Julia paused, hearing Mark clear his throat. She looked at him, leaning over the side of the pod. "May I help you, Mr. Henley?" she asked in feigned formality.

He gave her a quick look of warning, although he was grinning all the while. "Can I speak with you a minute?"

Julia nodded and followed Mark into his office.

"I'm going to have to postpone our dinner tonight," he said softly. "I've got a meeting and it's not going to let out early."

"All right," Julia replied, hiding her disappointment. She had been starting to look forward to a romantic dinner with Mark.

"Maybe Thursday night."

Julia nodded. "I think Thursday is okay."

"Me, too, but this is going to be a bad week."

"Well, whenever, Mark. We can have dinner any time." Julia folded her arms. "What's going on? Can you tell me?"

Mark sat on the corner of his desk, his one leg dangling over the side. "Bill decided to get rid of all the security staff and start from scratch. A memo will be circulated tomorrow, telling everyone about the change."

Julia was surprised. "Why?"

"Because the department was being run far too loosely and none of the employees seemed very eager to change their practices. Most of those guys are college students and thought this was a great job since they could do their homework while they worked. They weren't paying much attention to what was going on around them."

Julia was sorry to see a whole department go, and yet Mark's explanation made sense. He was a good business consultant, and she had come to respect his judgments.

"Frank Houston is going to train the new security officers," Mark added. "However, no one else here is aware that he works for the FBI. That's still 'top secret,' as they say."

"Oh, my." Julia grinned impishly. "Is a barbed wire fence going up around the building, too? That'll be great for the morale around here."

Rubbing the back of his neck, Mark chuckled. "No barbed wire." He shook his head at her. "You know, I can't figure out who's sassier . . . you or Stacie Rollins."

"Oh, it's Stacie, of course," Julia said facetiously. Then she rolled her eyes and left Mark's office with a broad smile.

The next morning, just as Mark had said, a memo was circulated stating that a whole new Security Department would be established.

"Hmm," Ken Driscoll said, leaning against Julia's pod, "I wonder which department is the next to go." He crumpled the memo and tossed it into a nearby wastebasket. "Must be nice to be a consultant. You wreak havoc and then go your merry way, never looking back at the damage you've done."

"I think the changes in security were Bill's idea," Julia stated in Mark's defense.

"But on whose suggestion?" Ken countered.

Julia didn't reply but marveled at the level of Ken's animosity toward Mark. She looked at her two new employees and wondered if they noticed it. By their expressions, she gathered they did.

"Well, my clients' money awaits," Ken said offhandedly. "Talk to you later."

As he walked away, Julia glanced at Mark's office door. She was glad it was closed because Mark still didn't like her talking to Ken, and she still couldn't avoid it.

Turning back to her employees, Julia smiled. "Shall we begin? We're going to get through two programs today."

Wednesday night was the mid-week worship service, and Julia was disappointed when Mark didn't make it. He said he had another meeting. Stacie came, however, and she sat with Julia, Jesse, Barb, and Glen. Stacie listened to the pastor intently, Julia noticed, and she even followed along when he read Scripture passages. She had purchased a Bible for her own use and it made Julia smile in satisfaction to see how reverently she handled her new treasure.

When Julia arrived home that night, the telephone was ringing. Jesse ran to answer it.

"It's Dad," he hollered from the next room. Then he took ten minutes to tell Mark every detail of his day.

Julia smiled as she listened, and then Jesse handed the telephone to her.

"Hi, Mark," she said jovially.

"Hi." His voice was flat. "Look, Juli, we heard some disturbing news today, and I asked Bill if I could be the one to confront you about it. He was agreeable."

"What is it?" she asked, sensing the seriousness of what was to come.

"Someone tried to make another illegal transaction today," Mark said. "It didn't go through from what we can find, but when we investigated further, another employee said she saw a woman in the CPU room." Mark paused. "She said it was you."

"Me? But I haven't been near the CPU room. Ask my employees. Except for an occasional trip to the ladies room, I've been with them all day."

"You were working with computer programs today?"

"Not working with them, Mark. I was paging through them . . . and my employees were there with me."

"All right." Mark's voice still sounded down and troubled.

"You don't believe me?"

She heard him let out a slow breath. "Juli, if you tell me that you weren't anywhere near the CPU room today, I believe you."

A moment's pause as they both digested questions and answers.

"Mark, who said that it was me?"

"Doesn't matter. The important thing is that she was wrong. Okay? I'm going to hang up now. Good night."

Julia heard the decisive click on the other end before turning off the portable phone. She wondered if Mark really believed her, but then realized that she couldn't do anything about the thoughts going around in his head right now. She had told him the truth, now he'd just have to trust her.

Trust her . . .

Julia got up from the chair she had been sitting in and walked to the patio windows. She pulled the draperies closed on the last of the setting sun. *With all odds against me, I'm insisting that Mark trust me. I haven't proven that I'm worthy of his trust. All I've given is my word. And yet, Mark has proved himself over and over. He's a different man. God changed his heart. It's obvious. But I still hold back on trusting him all the way.*

Julia shook her head sadly. She felt like a hypocrite, saying one thing, expecting another. And, ironically, she couldn't say that she'd blame Mark if he changed his mind about marrying her a second time.

At Weakland Management the next day, things were so tense on the third floor that Julia could barely concentrate. She considered taking the afternoon off, since her employees were doing well on their own; however, she was more than just a little intimidated about taking the idea to Bill. He looked preoccupied, serious, and very unapproachable.

Jerry Fein, on the other hand, seemed completely harassed. He walked briskly from one office to another, slamming doors and speaking loudly, and he glared at Julia each time he walked by. It occurred to her that if Mark was defending her, while Bill and Jerry thought she was guilty, he was putting his own reputation on the line. That troubled her. A lot.

Finally, five o'clock came, and Julia didn't waste a minute in gathering up her things and leaving. On the way out, she paused in front of Mark's office. "Good night," she ventured.

He looked up and smiled briefly. " 'Night, Juli."

Walking to the elevators, she thought of their plans for a "romantic dinner." But, given the day and Mark's expression just now, Julia knew it wouldn't be tonight.

As usual, she dined with Barb and Glen. Their love and friendship soothed Julia's misgivings over what was happening at work. She did, however, miss Mark's presence and Jesse, of course, wanted to know where his dad was and why he didn't come over tonight. Julia explained that he was having a busy week, and Jesse seemed satisfied with that. After all, his mother had had years of "busy weeks" in the past.

Once at home, with Jesse reading a book on the couch, Julia changed clothes and then sat outside on the patio with her Bible in her lap. The air was hot and humid, but it felt nice after being in cool air conditioning all day. She re-read this morning's devotional and Scripture application. One verse in particular stuck out at her: "A word fitly spoken is like apples of gold in pictures of silver."

Julia read it five times before deciding what to do with it. Re-entering the apartment she picked up the phone and dialed Mark's number. No answer. Then she tried him at his office, and found him.

"What's up, Juli?"

He sounded tired and Julia almost backed down from what she intended to say. Almost.

"I just called to tell you that . . . well, that I love you, Mark."

The words came straight from her heart — precious words, as precious as gold and silver. But, still, Julia held her breath, wondering over his reaction. This was the first time in twelve years that she reached out to Mark — without his prodding or prompting. It was all on her own.

"Thanks, Juli," he finally replied. "You'll never know how much it means to hear you say that. I'm glad you called."

She smiled, relieved. "Are you all right? You sound exhausted."

"I'll be fine . . . and I'm sorry for being such a bear lately. How's Jesse?"

"Terrific. He's reading a book."

"Wish I were reading a book."

Julia chuckled softly.

Mark heaved a weary-sounding sigh. "Do you have a few minutes? Can we talk?"

"Sure."

"All right. Tell me what you know about Angela Davis."

"Angela? Why?"

"Because she's the one who said it was you in the CPU room."

"Angela?"

"Uh-huh."

Julia paused to consider the news. It couldn't possibly be a case of mistaken identity; Angela knew very well what Julia looked like. So why would she lie?

"Tell me about her, Juli."

"Well, she's been with the company for almost a year. She's always been a big help to me. She even took the pager for me on a couple of weekends so that I could go to Jesse's soccer games and —"

"What did you say?"

"She took the pager for me . . ."

Realizing the implication of what she'd just said, Julia felt like her heart stood still. Hadn't the embezzler made the illegal transactions on the days when Julia was to have had the pager? But Angela had covered for her.

"This is all very interesting, isn't it?"

She sank onto the couch. "No, Mark, it's not Angela. She wouldn't steal money."

"Then why did she tell me that it was you in the CPU room?"

"I don't know."

"She didn't want me to tell you that she made the ID, either. Maybe she worried that we would talk to each other."

Julia was momentarily pensive. "You know, Mark, Angela told me that she caught you rummaging through my desk the very first Saturday you were here. I wasn't going to say anything to you because I figured it was just some mix-up."

Mark laughed. "Really? She said that? Funny thing, but I haven't worked a single Saturday since I came to Weakland Management." His voice grew serious. "All right, now we've got two blatant lies from Angela Davis."

"But she seems so sweet, Mark, and I really don't think she's capable of embezzling money."

"Maybe not . . . at least not on her own. But teamed with someone like . . . say, Ken Driscoll —"

"Ken and Angela?" Julia laughed. "No way! Besides, we already discussed Ken and —"

"And I always thought he was a shyster. Listen, Juli, in the six months he's worked for Weakland Management, Driscoll has stolen four accounts from other portfolio managers. What does that say about his character? Furthermore, Houston did background checks on every employee and Ken's is sketchy."

Julia didn't know what to say.

"There's something else. On one of my first days with Weakland Management, Ken told me that you were a . . . well, let's say he called you the company flirt."

"What!" Julia could only imagine the real terminology Ken had used. "You should have knocked him out — you still should! And if you don't, Mark, I will!"

He laughed. "You're in enough trouble. How about if we just figure out how to nail these two. I'm sure they're in it together. Angela had access to your PC, your desk —"

"My password, my initials." Julia sighed. "All my employees knew my codes. They had to in order to work on some of the data files."

"And then there's Driscoll who really did snoop through your desk. I saw him with my own eyes. And, as for Driscoll's trailing you everywhere when he should be paying attention to the Dow Jones average instead . . . well, nothing personal, honey, but I don't think he's really as smitten with you as he acts. I think he just wants to make sure that you haven't found out what he and Angela are up to."

"But it's so hard to believe. I feel . . . betrayed."

"I'm sure you do. But, Juli, you're going to have to overcome those feelings and help Houston prove that Angela and Ken are the real embezzlers."

"How?"

"I don't know," Mark said, his voice sounding weary once more. "I just don't know. But, Juli? Please be careful."

Chapter 21

Seven days later, Julia wiped the beads of perspiration off her forehead as she waited for Mark in the shade just outside the church's front doors. At seven o'clock, it was still a sultry eighty degrees on this first Wednesday evening in August.

"I got us a seat," Jesse said, coming to stand beside her now. "Are you sure Dad is coming?"

Julia nodded. "He said he had to work late, but he said he'd be here in time for the worship service."

Jesse nodded. "Hey, did Dad pop the question yet?"

"What question?" Julia replied, playing dumb.

"You know, *the question.*"

Julia shook her head. "Not yet." She grinned while Jesse frowned in disappointment. "You'll be the first to know, Jess. Not to worry."

He shrugged, his blond head now at

Julia's eye-level. Her son had grown a few inches in this summer's sunshine.

"Sam's mom said that she's never getting married again," Jesse confided. "She said she's having too much fun. I told her that you never had fun until Dad came along."

Julia had to laugh. "Thanks a lot, kid!" she teased him.

"Well, I didn't mean it in a bad way. I just mean that you're . . . happier now that he's here. You smile more . . . and you laugh more, too."

Julia agreed. "Yes, I am happier. I love your dad, that's true, but God is the One who put the joy back into my heart."

"Yeah, I told Sam's mom that part, too. Hey, look! Dad's here!"

Jesse ran out into the parking lot to meet Mark while Julia smiled in his wake. Then father and son walked back together.

"You guys sure are a sight for sore eyes!" Mark declared with a wink at Julia.

"Is that good or bad?" Jesse wanted to know.

"It's good. You and your mom are a good sight for my sore eyes." Mark chuckled.

"Anything new?" Julia asked hopefully as they walked into the vestibule. "How did your meeting go this afternoon?"

"No, and fine," Mark replied, answering both her questions. "We can talk later."

Julia nodded and slid into the pew next to Barb. In front of her, sitting beside Ryan Carlson, Stacie turned around. "Hello, Mark. Long time no see."

He grinned at the facetious remark. "Hi, Stacie." Then he nodded a friendly greeting to Ryan.

The pastor's message was short and then prayer requests were taken and testimonies given. Afterwards, the congregation was encouraged to break into small groups for prayer. Julia, Mark, and Jesse made up one group with Mark leading them through all the requests.

As she listened to him pray, Julia was awed by the depth of Mark's faith. His love for the Savior was obvious as first Mark praised Him, then thanked Him for an abundance of blessings, which included Julia and Jesse. Finally Mark interceded for other Christians, his words heartfelt, and an overwhelming sense of security enveloped Julia as she prayed along with him.

And at that very moment, she knew she could trust this man. She could trust him, because she trusted God — the same God who lived in Mark's heart!

★ ★ ★

The next morning at work, things seemed unusually tense. It wasn't like a busy stock-market-day tenseness. It was a quiet tenseness, like the calm before the storm.

Frank Houston was hanging around, going in and out of Bill's office, and Julia couldn't help but recall what Mark had said at breakfast. "Today's the day, Juli. I've just got the feeling . . ."

Julia hoped he was right. She hoped Houston would apprehend the thief, or thieves, very soon. She was getting nervous, working in such close proximity to Ken, and Julia had to constantly be aware of what she said or did so she wouldn't give the investigation away. On the more positive side, Bill didn't seem to distrust her anymore and even Jerry Fein was acting civil toward her again.

"Who is that man, Juli?" Ken asked, leaning his forearms on the wooden pod now. "I've seen him here before, but I thought he was just some flunky helping out Jerry Fein."

Julia pulled herself from her musings and wondered how to answer Ken's question without divulging the truth, but without lying either.

Finally, she said, "I don't know what his title is . . ."

"Hmm . . ." Ken's intense green-eyed gaze followed Houston as he picked up the telephone in Bill's office. Then he looked back at Julia and a softness entered his eyes. "I have to leave . . . a meeting . . ."

She nodded.

"Well, I . . ." He shrugged. "Good-bye, Juli."

She smiled. "Have a good day, Ken."

As he turned and walked back to his work area, a strange feeling came over Julia. Ken's good-bye had sounded so final.

Glancing across the way, Julia watched him pack up his attaché case. Then he looked around his desk as if making sure he hadn't forgotten anything. Nothing strange about that, since he'd said he had a meeting to attend. However, as Ken's gaze came back around to Julia, he gave her a slow, sad smile, and she immediately knew he was leaving for good. Fleeing, most likely.

Her eyes widened at the realization.

His gaze darkened in warning.

Oh, Lord, Ken knows I know . . .

Julia turned back to the training manual that she had been preparing for her newest

290

employee. Apprehension tingled her every nerve. She stared at the words in front of her, without seeing them, as she contemplated what to do next.

She glanced at Mark's office . . . empty. He was working with Public Relations this week. She looked over at Frank Houston. He was within shouting distance —

"Don't even think about it," Ken said softly, as he leaned over the pod and put his hand on Julia's shoulder. "I want you to stand up and follow me. Don't try anything stupid, because I have a gun and I'll use it."

She looked at him in wondering horror. "Ken . . . ?"

"Get up," he whispered.

She did, glancing at her two employees who were engaged in a conversation about computer components.

"Come on, Juli." Ken's tone was insistent now.

Hesitantly, she walked around the work area.

"Going for coffee?" one of her employees asked suddenly.

Julia opened her mouth to speak, but nothing came out.

"Mid-morning coffee break," Ken said with a forced smile. He looked at her. "Come on, Juli."

As she walked toward him, Julia wished she could come up with some clever way to get Frank Houston's attention. But she was so frightened, she couldn't even think. *Oh, Lord, please help me!*

Ken grabbed a hold of her upper arm, his impatience very evident now. "Move, Juli," he hissed, "I haven't got a lot of time."

He pulled her forward, and she had to run a few paces to get in time with his quick steps.

At the elevators, he released her arm. She rubbed it.

"I'm sorry," he said stiffly. "But just do as I say and everything will be fine, all right?"

Reluctantly, she nodded.

The elevator doors opened and Ken ushered her inside. Looking up at the camera in the left-hand corner, Julia wished that Bill hadn't fired all the security guards. One might have come in handy right about now.

She looked over at Ken who was watching her thoughtfully.

"How much do you know?" he asked.

Julia shrugged, but figured it was ridiculous to play dumb at this point. "I know that you tampered with my software and embezzled money."

A little smile curved Ken's mouth. "Took you long enough to figure it out."

Before Julia could reply, the elevator doors opened. They were on the first floor now. Using the phone just outside the Mail Room, Ken dialed a number and held the receiver to his ear, all the while holding Julia's hand. She wanted to pull out of his grasp, but she didn't know where he had the gun.

"It's time, Angie," Ken said into the phone. "Now!" Slamming down the receiver, he turned to Julia. "Come on. You're going to ensure our escape."

"What are you going to do with me?"

Ken smiled. "Once Angela and I are on our way out of the country, I'll let you go."

Julia sighed, praying she could believe him. "So Angela is really involved? I had hoped she wasn't."

Ken chuckled. "Angela is the mastermind behind all our plans."

Julia could barely believe it.

"We're married, you know."

"You and Angela?" Julia would have stopped dead in her tracks at the news, if Ken wasn't pulling her behind him. "But I thought Frank Houston did a background check on you and —"

Ken stopped so quickly that Julia almost

fell over him. "Who is Frank Houston?" His hand tightened around hers in a bone-breaking grip.

She winced. "He's with the FBI."

Ken muttered an oath. "I knew it!" He turned and kept walking, pulling Julia along with him. "I told Angela that I smelled trouble, but she just had to try one more transfer. She couldn't resist."

They reached the double-glass doors which led out to the parking lot and Ken leaned against the wall, waiting for Angela. Julia wiggled her hand out from under his.

He looked at her, but let her go.

Minutes passed, and Ken grew restless. After fifteen minutes, he was pacing the corridor like a caged animal. Finally, Angela appeared, although she was standing out in the parking lot. Just standing there. With her hands behind her back.

"What in the world . . . ?" Ken grabbed Julia's elbow and pushed her through the doors. "What are you doing out there?" he shouted to Angela. "I was waiting for you in —"

"Watch out, Ken!" she cried. "Run!"

The next seconds were a blur of shouts and shuffling feet as, first, Frank Houston grabbed hold of Angela's arm, though she was already handcuffed, and two other men took Ken down, handcuffing him. This left Julia standing in the middle of the chaos, feeling stunned and more than just a little frightened.

Finally, when Ken and Angela were loaded into a waiting car, Houston approached her.

"You okay?"

Julia just stared back at him, dumbstruck.

"I realized you were in trouble," he explained, "when I saw Driscoll holding you by the arm and leading you toward the elevators. I summoned my men and we got to Angela before she could get away. She was amazingly compliant. We used her as bait, so to speak, in order to apprehend Driscoll. Worked out nicely, I think." Houston narrowed his gaze. "Are you sure you're all right, Miss McGowan?"

She managed a nod, although she felt as if she had just gotten off a spinning ride at an amusement park.

"Would you like to sit down?"

"I'll be all right."

And then she saw Mark. He was running toward her from around the other side of the building. Seeing her, he paused, taking in the outcome of the situation. But then he closed the distance between them, pulling Julia into his arms.

"Thank God you're not hurt," he said, his lips brushing against her ear. "When Bill told me what was happening, I . . . I panicked, Juli. I don't know what I would have done if something happened to you."

Julia wanted to tell him that he was holding her too tightly — that she couldn't breathe. But she just as soon decided that she'd gladly die in Mark's arms this way. He loved her and she was unharmed. God had answered her prayers.

"It's a beautiful night, isn't it?" Mark said as they strolled along Lake Michigan's breakwater walkway. Two weeks had gone by since Ken and Angela had been arrested and changed with theft.

Julia nodded in answer to Mark's question. It was a beautiful night. The temperature was mild here by the lake, and a sliver of moon shone in the sky surrounded by hundreds of stars. "Beautiful."

"Dinner was good, don't you think?"

"Very good."

Julia bit the inside of her cheek in an effort to suppress her giggles. Poor Mark. He had been making small talk all night when what he so obviously wanted to do was "pop the question."

"That was a very elegant restaurant," Mark said. "I'm glad you suggested it."

"Me, too. I had never been there before."

"What was the name of that place again?"

"Pieces of Eight." Julia smiled, wondering if she should help Mark out. They could go on like this all night.

Deciding she ought to, she strategically slipped her hand into his. "It was very romantic, Mark. The candlelight, the view of the lake as we ate . . ."

He nodded, and Julia could feel the clamminess on the palm of his hand. *He's nervous. How sweet!*

They reached the end of the walkway and Mark turned to her. Julia could clearly see his features beneath the soft glow of the street lamp several feet away. She watched as he seemed to struggle with what he wanted to say. Then he took a deep breath.

"You're not going to throw me in the lake, are you?" she teased, trying to put him at ease.

"No, not tonight," Mark said seriously, in spite of her attempt at humor. He took another preparatory breath, and Julia bit the inside of her cheek again. *Don't laugh. Don't even smirk.*

Her mirth faded, however, as she remembered that Mark didn't have this much trouble proposing twelve years ago. *He's serious this time,* she realized. *This is forever, and he knows it.*

"I love you, Juli," he said, taking both her hands in his as he leaned against the painted, metal rail behind him.

"I love you, too."

Mark nodded. "I know . . . and I've been doing a lot of thinking about . . . us."

"Yes?"

"And Jesse. I mean . . . I've been thinking about what's best for all of us."

Julia nodded, wishing he'd just spit it out.

"I'm leaving for Colorado after Christmas, and —"

"You are?"

Mark nodded. "Look, Juli," he said, sounding more like his old practical self. "I need a business partner, okay? I want someone organized, intelligent, educated and, well, you fit the bill."

"Business partner?" she asked in disbelief. "You want a . . . *a business partner?*"

"We'd make a great team, don't you think?"

"Well, yes, but —"

"You'll travel with me and . . . well, we could see each other all the time — have romantic moon-lit walks like this every night if we want to. And I could see Jesse all the time —"

"Business partner?" Julia's ire was up now. So he wasn't talking commitment. He was talking — "Business partner!" She yanked her hands free.

"Well, there is just one condition."

With arms akimbo now, she glared at him. "And what might that be?"

"You'd have to marry me." Mark grinned.

Julia blinked. He got her. He got her good, and he knew it. Mark laughed and laughed.

"Very funny," she said dryly.

"I'm sorry, Juli," he said between chortles, "I couldn't help myself."

And here she had tried so hard not to laugh at him!

Folding her arms in front of her, she allowed Mark to chuckle it out. Finally, he grew serious again.

"I'm sorry I teased you. But you see, I just had to lighten up the moment. I was getting too nervous in all the seriousness." Mark paused, swallowing hard. "Except, I am serious. Will you marry me, Juli?"

"You going to show up this time?"

Mark looked chagrined. "I knew you were going to say that." He grinned. "Yes, I'll show up this time. I promise."

"You know what, Mark? I believe you. And I trust you. Completely."

Then, an earnest expression on his face, he got down on his knees. "Juli, I promise you forever — as much of forever as God allows me to give. Will you marry me?"

Julia's heart melted at the sight. "Yes," she replied, "I'll marry you."

Epilogue

December 21

The church in Menomonee Falls, Wisconsin, was modestly, but tastefully decorated. Fresh floral arrangements stood in glass vases near the altar and pleated paper wedding bells, in a variety of pastels, hung about. The pews were filled with enthusiastic friends and relatives who had come to share this special day. A wedding day, uniting for life Julia Rose McGowan and Mark Thomas Henley.

In the dressing room in back of the church, Julia smoothed the skirt of her formal off-white, tea-length gown which she'd purchased especially for this day.

"You look beautiful, dear," Julia's mother, Caroline, said with a proud smile. Then tears gathered in her green eyes. "You're the most beautiful bride I've ever seen."

"Oh, Mom, don't cry," Julia chided her

gently. "You'll ruin your makeup. Don't forget pictures afterward in the Mitchell Park Domes."

Caroline nodded, dabbing her eyes with a tissue.

Then, as if tears were contagious, Barb dabbed at her eyes, too. "This is one happy day," she muttered. Then to Julia she said, "You once asked what you could do to payback Glen and me for all the years you lived with us. Well, honey, this wedding is all the pay-back I'll ever need or want. You and Mark . . . oh, it's so wonderful to see what God can do!"

"Thank you, Barb," Julia said, giving her a hug. "Thank you so much."

"You're welcome. Now, smooth your hair and let me fix your veil. I think I bumped it."

Turning around, Julia allowed Barb to fuss over her for a few minutes.

"You do make a beautiful bride, Juli," Kathy said sweetly.

Julia smiled her thanks. She and Kathy hadn't seen each other in over twelve years, but when Julia phoned her, it was as if they'd never been apart — best friends once more. Kathy, her husband, and four children had come up from Illinois for the wedding.

"And the gown is stunning, Juli," Stacie said, handing her a pair of pearl earrings. "But these will make the whole outfit."

Julia took the earrings and smiled. "Thank you, Stacie. How thoughtful."

"Well, aren't you supposed to have something borrowed and something blue? Those earrings are borrowed, Juli, and I want them back before you leave for Colorado."

Julia laughed. "Good as done."

"So what are you going to do with Jesse?" Kathy asked. "All that traveling Mark does, and your going with him . . . what about Jesse's education?"

Julia smiled. "I'm going to home-school," she announced. "I'll be Jesse's teacher, and he'll be able to study anywhere we go. I'm excited about it."

Mark's sisters, Teri and Jenny, stood by and smiled. They had come for the wedding with their spouses and children, too.

"Next to Teri," Jenny remarked, "I couldn't ask for a better sister than you, Juli."

Now Julia's eyes grew misty. She hugged Jenny. "I love you. I really do." Then she embraced Teri. "You, too."

"This should have happened a long time ago," Teri said, teary eyed.

But Julia shook her head. "God knew what He was doing. Mark and I had to give our lives to Him before we could give our lives to each other."

Teri nodded, wiping away her emotion.

Peggy Henley suddenly stuck her head into the dressing room. "Everybody ready?" She smiled at Julia. "Oh, darling, you look gorgeous!"

"She'd better," Stacie said facetiously. "We've been working on her for two hours!"

All the ladies laughed and any melancholy vanished.

"I can't wait to see Mark's face when you walk up the aisle," his mother said. Her white-blond hair was pinned elegantly in a chignon, and her emerald green dress accentuated a rosy hue that all the excitement had put into her cheeks.

The prelude sounded and Peggy's eyes grew wide. "That's the cue. Time to go."

They all left the dressing room and stood in the vestibule while the "mothers" — all three of them — took their places in the front pew. They were the last to be ushered forward by Julia's brothers before the wedding procession began.

The matron of honor, Kathy, walked up the aisle with Tim, Mark's older brother.

Next, Teri with her husband, and then Jenny with hers. Stacie followed, escorted by Dr. Brent McDonald, a long-time friend of Mark's and, finally, Jesse, the ring bearer, made his way to the altar.

Taking her father's arm, Julia smiled. "You look great, Dad."

He was beaming. "You're not so bad yourself." Roy cleared his throat. "I'm proud of you, Juli, and I'm proud of Mark. Oh, and he wanted me to tell you something."

Julia lifted a brow. "Uh-oh. I don't know —"

Roy chuckled. "You'll want to hear this, I think." He paused momentarily, collecting his thoughts. "I accepted Christ as my Savior, Juli. Mark and your brother Rick talked to me and I saw my need . . ."

"Oh, Dad, that's wonderful!" Julia couldn't contain her happiness and threw her arms around her dad's thick neck.

"Easy now, honey, you'll wrinkle my tux."

Julia let him go. "Sorry about that." She straightened his lapels.

And then it was their turn to go forward.

Step by step, they walked up the aisle as cameras flashed and friends and family smiled. All Julia could see was Mark, waiting for her and wearing an expression that bordered on awe and anticipation. He was the most handsome man she'd ever seen.

Stepping around her, Roy "gave her away," slipping Julia's hand into Mark's elbow. Then the vows were spoken, the promises made. A commitment for a lifetime. They were united as man and wife.

"You may kiss your bride," the pastor said with a good-natured grin.

Mark smiled at her and Julia's knees grew weak. "I've been waiting a long time to do this," he murmured, his lips touching hers. Then he kissed her with a passion that Julia felt to the tips of her toes, and the congregation applauded.

"Allow me to present," the pastor said, "Mr. and Mrs. Mark Henley."

About the Author

Andrea Boeshaar has been married for twenty-five years. She and her husband, Daniel, have three adult sons. Andrea attended college, first at the University of Wisconsin-Milwaukee, where she majored in English, and then at Alverno College, where she majored in Professional Communications and Business Management.

Andrea has been writing stories and poems since she was a little girl; however, it wasn't until 1984 that she started submitting her work for publication. In 1991 she became a Christian and realized her calling to write exclusively for the Christian market. Since then Andrea has written articles, devotionals, and over a dozen novels for *Heartsong Presents* as well as numerous novellas for Barbour Publishing. In addition to her own writing, she works as an agent for Hartline Literary Agency.

When she's not at the computer, Andrea enjoys being active in her local church and taking long walks with Daniel and their "baby" — a golden Labrador-Retriever mix named Kasey.

The employees of Thorndike Press hope you have enjoyed this Large Print book. All our Thorndike and Wheeler Large Print titles are designed for easy reading, and all our books are made to last. Other Thorndike Press Large Print books are available at your library, through selected bookstores, or directly from us.

For information about titles, please call:

(800) 223-1244

or visit our Web site at:

www.gale.com/thorndike
www.gale.com/wheeler

To share your comments, please write:

Publisher
Thorndike Press
295 Kennedy Memorial Drive
Waterville, ME   04901